SONGS MY MOTHER NEVER TAUGHT ME

SELÇUK ALTUN

SONGS MY MOTHER NEVER TAUGHT ME

Translated from Turkish by
Ruth Christie and Selçuk Berilgen

TELEGRAM
London   San Francisco   Beirut

ISBN: 978-1-84659-053-5

First published in Turkish as *Annemin Öğretmediği Şarkılar*
by Sel Yayincilik, Istanbul, Turkey

This English translation published by Telegram, 2008

Copyright © Selçuk Altun, 2008
English translation copyright © Ruth Christie, 2008

Cover photograph: *Closing* by Robert Taylor (detail);
© Istockphoto.com

Manufactured in Lebanon

TELEGRAM
26 Westbourne Grove, London W2 5RH
825 Page Street, Suite 203, Berkeley, California 94710
Tabet Building, Mneimneh Street, Hamra, Beirut
www.telegrambooks.com

A

My mother, the most fearless woman I'd ever known, had succumbed to cancer. After seven weeks in the hospital so charmingly named after Florence Nightingale, she died. Her final words before entering Intensive Care had been, 'They say the best döner kebab house in Istanbul is on the street to the right of this building. Go and try it, Arda ...'

To anyone reading the script on my parents' headstone, which was on the plot next to the poet Oktay Rifat, they might have seemed like father and daughter:

Prof. Dr. Mürsel Kemal Ergenekon (1928–1991)
Prof. Dr. Ada Ergenekon (1950–2003)

I waited seven days before breaking up with Jale, queen of dilemmas, who compared herself to the film star Julia Roberts and was a sociology student at an American

university with an absurd name. Liberated from this
wealthy girl I'd got engaged to merely to please my
mother, I was savouring belated pride like a high-school
student heading to a brothel for the first time.

In the Ottoman mansion where I've lived as its heir,
guest, prisoner, and now master, I enjoy the excitement
of not knowing how many days or years I'll remain. For
İfakat's sake – the tireless servant of a tired old building
who'd swallow a stale prostate pill so it wouldn't be wasted
– I haven't taken refuge in my apartment at the top of a
skyscraper in central but quiet Şişli. As the shutters' futile
struggle with the south wind ends, the morning ezan
begins. I wait patiently in the drawing room, surrounded
by bronze statuettes. When the prayer ends the wind will
assail again. My left hand enjoys shaking cigar ash onto the
silk carpet, and I realize I've forgotten what kind of drink
is in my right. At the funeral service attended by the élite
of the city I had murmured lines from Küçük İskender's
Rock Manifesto,[1] and now I can hum that cruel tirade until
I pass out in the dim morning hours. Today I am twenty-

[1] Smear me with eczema, Mother! O Mother, sell me a sedative!
Buy me a treasure map! Hire me a warning siren; give me back my
umbilical cord, Mother; warm me milk and menstrual blood and
cook me rakı; bring me up dissolute; offer me so many hormones
and enzymes! Bite me, Bitch-Mother! Be the bass-guitarist to
the Iron Maiden. Go and train in guerrilla warfare and take to
the mountains! Start a firing squad for shooting rows of children!
Grow up, Mother, and leave my penis in peace! With it I'll ensure
credit from the sperm banks!

seven years old. And the only gift I desire is the ecstasy of being liberated from my mother and my fiancée.

B

According to Ebu Musa el-Eş'ari, Our Lord the Prophet has announced:

'On the Day of Judgement Muslims will come laden with sins and Allah will still forgive them.'

Today your humble servant Bedirhan Öztürk is thirty-seven years old! Instead of buying myself a birthday present I've come to a crucial decision. God willing, I'm going to break away from the business I've undertaken so patiently for the last twelve years.

Please don't let the fact that I'm a hired killer alarm you. My mission was limited to those who'd committed deadly crimes, particularly against our religion, and dared to hide in the cracks of our system of justice and security. God knows I haven't taken more than two lives a year.

And in a country where it is claimed that for every 100 lira paid in tax 225 lira are lost through tax evasion, I donate a fortieth of my income to the orphans and the fatherless.

When I first took up with the trade I was warned that it was hard to enter the world of bullets but even harder to get out. A revolting individual (who goes by the name of Baybora) would pass on the Head Executioner's orders to me.

'Don't even think about early retirement! You'd have to take out the Boss first,' he'd threaten.

I've never even heard our Master's voice, let alone seen his face.

But retirement will come to pass, by the grace of God! Listening reverently to the evening ezan and eating my blessed pomegranate, I'll say my prayers and go to sleep, if you'll allow me. I'm sure you've already begun to realize that your humble servant is no ordinary gun-toting operator.

A

How often my mother had boasted that there couldn't be any mansion more elevated than ours, or with a better view of Istanbul. I used to trace the panoramic mosaic of the city, square by square, and the strategic points that seemed to be waiting their turn for a march past of history. Despite the barricade of mist, a Byzantine residue, I would flirt with the towers of Topkapı Palace, and when a lazy breeze drifted over the stone wall it would carry a fresh smell of garden herbs into the drawing room and die away in a sigh.

She said she chose Çamlıca, which draws the morning ezan from the 3,000 city mosques like a magnet, because 'there's no neighbourhood left that hasn't lost its flavour'. She made her father buy her a wedding present of the

Ottoman mansion with its symmetrical façade and ornate carvings.

'As soon as I saw Mürsel I was determined to have him as my lord and master,' she would eagerly confide. 'As he walked around the campus biting his lower lip, hands in the pockets of his crumpled trousers, even the left-wing girl students trembled. He played hard to get alright, but those condescending little smiles of his were enough to charm people, and despite his oily hair and his unseemly scratching at certain organs, even the women cleaners admired him ...'

Unfortunately my mother was an attractive woman with her abundant blonde hair, eyes blue as the sea, her turned-up nose and her shapely figure. I thought that even the street dogs would stop and stare as she walked by. When we went to the market together I wanted my toy gun to zap all those shabby men whose eyes were glued to her.

I mustn't enter into the flirtatious details of how she brought her husband to the boil. But while my father was busy divorcing 'the barren first wife whose teaching diploma no one had ever seen' and whom he had married 'under orders from his aunt', I can just whisper how Tilda Taragano changed her name and religion to gain access to her lord and master.

My mother's father, Izak Taragano, was a Sephardic Jew. While studying law at the University of Geneva, he fell in love at first sight with Anna, a student who was taller than him. For twenty-seven months he begged his mother for permission to marry the attractive girl who was a philosophy student from Stockholm and the daughter of a couple of Christian atheist academics. On 7 April 1947, the day when Henry Ford, founder of the motor industry died, my grandmother gave birth to a paralysed male child, and her neurotic mother-in-law grumbled, 'The cold-eyed Viking dybbuk'.[1]

My uncle Salvador dragged his left leg from the hip as he walked. I never saw such a saintly person.

My mother and Princess Anne of Great Britain were 'privileged' to be born on 15 August 1950, under 'the sign of Leo'. She was named Tilda, after the wife of the eminent writer Yaşar Kemal, my grandmother's confidante. When she was little, my mother was headstrong and greedy, but pretty as a doll, and she became the family mascot, beloved by her father's mother who called her 'the dybbuk fawn'. She graduated from the American Girls' College at Üsküdar, second in the whole school, and was steered in the direction of Brandeis, the favoured university of young Jewish girls, by Tilda Kemal. While my father was professor in the Mathematics department of Boğaziçi University, she was studying for her doctorate in the department of English Language and Literature. I was seven years old when they bought me a bicycle because I could rattle off the title of her thesis, 'The Indirect Influence of Elias Canetti in the Novels of Iris Murdoch'. She was preparing this

---

1   A mischievous wandering djinn in Jewish folklore which takes over a human soul until driven out by prayer.

under the supervision of Professor Oya Başak, one of the rare academics she considered important. The family did not approve of her marriage to a professor who was old, a widower and a Muslim, but raised no objection, realizing it would fall on deaf ears.

When I was still a baby crawling on all fours, my grandmother died of cancer. Whenever I look at her photograph on the birchwood coffee table in our drawing room I note with surprise how much she resembles my mother on her deathbed.

After her death my grandfather and uncle found themselves within my mother's orbit once again.

Cʒ

My mother's womb was torn at my birth and had to be removed. I thought she was subconsciously taking her revenge by imprisoning me in her palace of detention.

(I felt proud if, in a dream, I said, 'Hey, Mother, how come you never noticed how you shoved the son you worried about so much into such a vortex of distress?') I was as shy and docile as a prince and heir apparent in exile. I was wealthy but captive in the midst of decisions and vetoes made in my name.

My mother didn't stop at deciding which toy I should play with and when; she forbade me to have friends. 'I can be much funnier than them, Arda,' she would say with feeling. And I was bewitched by the fantastic stories she whispered. The modulations of her magical voice, her artificial chuckle and threatening eye movements took over my life. On the two half-days she went to the university she was happy if I cried when she left. Apparently as the garden gate closed behind the huge Mercedes, I beat at İfakat's huge breasts and bit her snow-white arms neurotically.

When I was in the second year of my primary school the driver of the school minibus was sacked for scolding me. The following year a bad-tempered teacher who tried to punish me for an April Fool joke that he didn't appreciate was banished to a distant village. In the preparatory class at Robert College a young thug pinched my cheek, jeering that I was prettier than a girl, and I knew that next day he would get a beating from Hayrullah our driver and his twin. Then Seydo the neighbourhood bully, who didn't know what he was letting himself in for, bellowed after me, 'Secret Jew', and was thrashed to a pulp, his father's dried-fruit store reduced to dust and ashes, and his family forced to leave Çamlıca.

On Sunday evenings our family would trot off to a Bosphorus fish restaurant. While my mother chatted with the hoi polloi at the next table, I fed the resident cat seabass in Soy sauce, and I never let the evening pass without boasting that my mother could make me walk on water if I asked her.

ख

My mother always addressed her husband as 'my Hodja',

a respectful form of address to a senior teacher. He was one of the twentieth century's leading mathematicians, 'unmatched in Graph Theory' according to his former student and the bibliophile Professor Haluk Oral, whom I met after my father's death. My father published in the *Journal of Combinatorial Theory* but his timidity (and fear of flying) led him to refuse offers of guest professorships and participations in international conferences. I think my mother devoted herself to publicizing my father's genius. I was torn: should I be jealous of her exaggerated interest in my father or feel sorry for him? Every time she whispered in my ear, 'You're very fortunate to be the son of a genius,' I would repeat my vow that I would never be a genius when I grew up. When my father became eligible for retirement and, thanks to his wife, rose to the ranks of the rich, he left his job immediately.

'An all-out war against the socio-economic defect of shallowness that sticks to this country like tar,' was the Hodja's new mission. My mother whispered it distinctly in my ear, and promised me a prize of $100 for repeating it without a mistake. Reverently she said, 'Arda, your father is a genius and a man of eminence. From now on, he will mobilize all his abilities for this grand project.'

The structure of our nuclear family life was determined by the tempo of my father's activities. It took order to the nth degree. I felt ill at ease every time he emerged from his soulless study to join us. As the creaky old door of the living room opened, my mother would jump up to push the velvet pouffe in front of his antique armchair. Baroque music was set up on the hi-fi and, while his drink was being prepared, he remained silent. Unnecessary or perhaps trivial subjects would be rejected and a new agenda respectfully anticipated.

'Enigma', the silent hairdresser, came to our mansion when our master's hair grew too long. Fabrics chosen by my mother were made into suits and if the head tailor of Zegna's was in town he would drop by for fittings. On holidays celebrating the Republic my mother and I took off for London and went to concerts and plays. She grumbled at having to shop in Harrods and in Bond Street boutiques for the husband who couldn't or wouldn't join us for fear of flying. If religious holidays coincided with spring our family took a trip to Venice. Walking rapidly through the time-warp streets of this solitary city, bridge after bridge, my father, if he wasn't solving equations, would be composing theorems. We stayed at the Bauer Hotel, the secluded palace in St Mark's Square; if Cimador, Dragonetti, Lorenzetti or Bottesini were being performed, we would stroll to the charming Church of San Vitale. (How is it I recall these marginal composers of classical music in whom my mother feigned an interest because my father had such a passion for them? Ever since I was seven I haven't forgotten a single name I've read. My father's cheap display of genius was due to his ability to multiply five-digit numbers in his head with the speed of a computer. I don't know if anyone else can do this, but ever since I got the hang of the four basic operations of arithmetic, I've been able to tackle six-digit numbers. I concealed this meaningless gift of mine which would have been offensive to my father and would have roused my mother to an ecstasy of pride.)

Thanks to my mother's unfailing attentions, my father turned into a querulous gourmand. Favourite foods were specially ordered – fresh halloumi from Kyrenia, lean pastrami from Kayseri, mildly hot sausage from Afyon, hazelnuts double-roasted from Giresun and spicy chickpeas from Çorum. Tea and jam were procured from Fortnum & Mason in London, pastries and sauces from Fauchon in Paris. My mother had even learned how to serve a cheese omelette Café les Deux Magots style. If there was a special order of oven-cooked Sicilian pizza from Il Pomodoro (London), or extra-tender veal from Peter Luger (New York), they were met at the airport and ceremoniously rushed to the mansion like life-saving medicines.

My father, who couldn't ride a bicycle let alone drive a car, confessed that, 'rather than fight a duel with a computer', he preferred to just get on with his work longhand.

He couldn't swim or sunbathe by the pool. He was nervous of miniature dogs and sleepy cats and electronic instruments. It irked me when, tired of the TV channel he was watching, and too lazy even to lean over to reach for the remote control, he'd shout to my mother, frantically busy in the kitchen. Sometimes I wondered if he even pulled the chain after relieving himself. I was sure that when they made love my mother was twice as exhausted. It seemed his mechanical inadequacy was 'the sublime characteristic that separated his genius from the rest'.

I was sure that even if my father had been twenty-eight instead of forty-eight at my birth, we would never have had a close relationship. He was not loving. A certain attitude to those around him seemed to indicate that you owed him respect for sharing the same time zone with you. His merciless wit would wound anyone who talked nonsense. He was tall, green-eyed, attractive and cynical. I liked to compare him to John le Carré, master of the Cold War spy thriller. If I was the nightingale in a gold cage, caught in the spiral of my mother's house arrest, he was the rare exotic fish in an aquarium made for one.

The Master, as his wife called him, was the only man who could gather under one roof fragmented Social Democrats and disgruntled right-wing intellectuals. He even had a plan to raise the level of prosperity in their unfortunate country to that of Spain within five years, and to become Prime Minister in the first general election.

On the eve of my fourteenth birthday we received the news of my father's death. After the first shock I had to prepare myself for what was to come.

 CR

While I was busy concealing my potential genius my mother continued hissing like a snake for three years,

'When my son finishes high school he'll enrol in business studies at Harvard.'

I was accepted by Harvard with the help of influential teachers at my school, references from famous friends of my father and my mother's efforts, and I was happy for her. But when she had the tabloids print simplistic headlines like, 'Harvard Chosen for Top Professor's Son,' she became, from that moment, the object of my disdain.

If I didn't call her twice a day in my first year her partially suppressed anger would find me out at the oddest hours to extract a verbal report. To stop her flying over at once and picking a quarrel with my tutors, I had to make 90 per cent grades. Unfortunately, the summer I passed into the second year she was appointed Project Consultant at Harvard. We were to spend an intimate spell of two terms in a pile of bricks called a villa overlooking the River Charles in the campus city of Cambridge. In the remaining years that seemed to last for ever, while guest lecturer Ada Ergenekon was teaching comparative literature in her pretentious English, I was overwhelmed by depression.

I'd even prepared myself for the possibility of an American stepfather, as a way of escaping her irritating attentions. But, as she declared to the media world, 'she could think only of her one and only Arda.' She made provocative use of dress, speech and body language to keep the men around her under control. I was furious when she flirted subconsciously with friends who came to see me. And with her artificial sincerity, subtlety and powerful mind games she was constantly trying to wear down my poor girlfriends.

My mother held various trading companies under the umbrella of the Taragano Financial Services, of which she was one of three partners. My grandfather, chairman of the board of directors, was uneasy with Uncle Salvador, his assistant, who was behaving honestly and failing to increase corporate profits. He would tickle my nose with his amber rosary beads and say, 'Finish your schooling, for goodness sake, then we'll make a killing and share it between us.'

My great-great-grandfather had risen into the wealthy class through his black-market profiteering on basic foodstuffs. As for my grandfather, on the eve of the military intervention of 12 September 1980, he'd been involved in smuggling gold and then turned his hand to fictitious exports and pilfered government tax returns, thereby making a profit of $150,000,000 in the process, only to regret that 'we missed the big one!'

My mother's shares were transferred to my name after I graduated with honours from Harvard, but I knew she wouldn't allow me to move to the high-rise flat my grandfather had given me. She'd also rebuked my uncle for buying me a sports car.

My world darkened that summer night I heard of Iris Murdoch's terminal illness while I was driving along the Bosphorus. My mother later reported that 'the minibus that hit your Ferrari from behind flew into the sea at

Yeniköy and the pervert driver with his Slav slut are now feeding the fish.' I remember my inner organs shifting at the moment of impact. As I was gradually sliding down that dark tunnel perhaps I smiled at the consoling thought that sooner or later my mother would drag me out into the light. I had severe head injuries and was subsequently admitted for surgery and diagnosed with acute subdural haematosis. Despite a successful operation, and because of the possibility of chronic bleeding, I was flown to the Mayo Clinic in Rochester, USA, in an ambulance plane brought from Switzerland. It seems a second operation was performed to prevent blood accumulating between the brain cells. For seven months I wrestled with visual and speech difficulties, partial memory loss and, most embarrassing of all, incontinence. I recall only half-seeing my mother and being unable to remember if my name came from a river or a lake. If she wasn't beside me when I woke, I'd hear her crying in the next room and start to worry. A doctor of Tartar origin conveyed to me in his broken Turkish that if it hadn't been for my mother not only would a quick recovery be out of the question, but I'd probably have remained partially disabled. During my convalescence I'd longed in vain to be rid of my cerebral talents. I vowed, as we boarded the New York–Istanbul flight, that I would never ever again upset *my saintly mother.*

CR

As the noon ezan ended and before her ghost entered the scene, I had to throw the cigar butt that had fallen on the floor into the Ottoman ashtray. My mother's soul was even capable of arriving uninvited while I was wrestling with whatever old bottle of booze was at hand. Then I could wonder if she'd put the Tartar doctor up to that last compliment.

I can't just invent a shower of autumn rain as in trashy novels and then drop off to sleep. Instead, I'll doze off humming a passage from Küçük İskender's *Rock Manifesto*[1] ...

---

[1] While I weep in my room, take a shower in blood, Mother! Warm me up milk and menstrual blood! Please don't be startled if I howl to the full moon, don't be angry with my friend the devil for staying over now and then, don't be angry with him having an orgasm and yelling, '666 666' as he urinates in the toilet ... you sing and dance, Mother, while others are being murdered! Clean my weapons, oil them! Don't even try to understand why I masturbate till dawn! We are alone, all of us alone. I know it's very funny, but now it's time for you too to learn this, Mother!

B

Our Lord the Prophet read the following prayer for
Hasan and Hüseyin, his grandsons:
'Lord God! I seek refuge in nurturing words, against
all humankind, djinns, devils, all harmful things and
the evil eye.'

Buhari: *Tecrid-i sarih*, 1348

I confess I'm the poet who wrote the following graffiti on
the wall: 'How can I yearn for tears when I haven't been
given a taste for laughter?' and: 'Show me the poor soul
who has never been victimized first by his own family!'

My master Baki, may he dwell in paradise, uttered the
words, 'How can the Four Sacred Books fit into a single
volume if they're not more poetically precise than *Hamlet*?'
In the first twenty-five years of my life – shall I see a

23

second? – spent struggling to survive, I couldn't even enjoy my unhappiness to the full. If your humble servant is not to upset you with episodes from his naive youth, he must get down to the nitty-gritty of the psychological make-up of his soul.

As my ancestors were a mixture of Kurdish Yazidi and Arab Christian, who lived at N. on the Syrian border, it's clear why they took the surname 'Öztürk'.[1] My great-grandfather wasn't from a noble tribe and was saved from poverty by smuggling live animals and imperishable foodstuffs. He had a folk song composed in his honour after he happened to shoot a famous army captain in self-defence. On the eve of the holy Kurban festival, while he was out foraging, news arrived that he'd been blown to bits in a minefield.

They say that my grandfather, a janitor in the Public Registry Office, was overjoyed when eventually a son, Vahit, was born after four daughters. Vahit attended primary school for six years and middle school for five and, returning from military service, ran away to Istanbul with Piraye, a student from the teachers' training college. She was the only daughter of a director from Urla who had come to N. as a left-wing exile and womanizer, and when he disowned his daughter and banished his future in-laws to the Bulgarian border, the town was rife with rumours. My namesake grandfather died of a heart attack and his family scattered.

---

1   A genuine Turk, from *öz* (real) and *Türk* (Turk).

It seemed to me I came into the world at the age of four in Tarlabaşı, the very navel of Istanbul, and didn't mind if the crazy taxi-drivers and street vendors underestimated our kaleidoscopic streets. I saw hopeless women relaxing at their ramshackle windows, scolding their kids in heavily accented Turkish or Kurdish. If no quarrelsome voices arose from the rotting front of a building it was blacklisted as 'eccentric'. We sheltered in resigned companionship, the common denominator of absolute poverty.

My father would return home at dusk and I'd prepare to shut my ears to the inevitable row. He beat my mother until she took refuge in my room, embracing me and crying, 'My poor son', but somehow her sobs and trembling failed to move me.

My father was head bouncer at the notorious Wo-Manhattan Night Club. My mother shot him and his gypsy dancer mistress, and then committed suicide, leaving me to the care of seventy-year-old Marika Anadolyadis on the ground floor.

My mother had dubbed Marika the original Queen of Tarlabaşı, as she emerged into İstiklal Street wearing her violent redskin warpaint and her gear that was thirty years out of date. In her flat, which resembled a warehouse of museum pieces, she distracted me by reading detective stories.

Our lumpen neighbourhood spokesman grew irritated with this funny woman who was cinema-obsessed and always reading to the accompaniment of classical music.

Declaring that 'this hunchback dwarf will ruin my adopted nephew', he decided that I must be taken away from her. I remember hugging Marika and crying for one last time in my dark cellar that reeked of detergent. Through the intervention of my late father's tough patron I was placed in the Kasımpaşa Education Institute for Orphans and put in the fourth year of the primary school. The arrival of your humble servant was the most momentous event in the history of this public institution that housed orphans and the poor. I was shunned as though I had murdered my parents.

Later, at the Artisan School of Printing, also for orphans, I knew that my tragic fame would leak out at registration time and that within forty-eight hours the whole school would be full of rumours. I learned not to take offence at the feigned compassion of the teachers. I wasn't popular in the dormitory on account of my great love of books and my taciturn nature. But at the beginning of every year I had a period of peace after I made a public demonstration of beating up the first unwary fellow who wasn't deterred by my bulk.

The teachers at the school were as poor and unhappy as the children. Many collapsed with exhaustion after the extra work they took on to make ends meet. Books became my only friends, and I read every one in the school library. For this I was regarded as eccentric. I dreamt of becoming a secondhand bookseller who enjoyed the aroma of the books and was consumed, sentence by sentence, sucked into the whirlpool. The job that would threaten my solitude least was perhaps that of a lighthouse keeper. (Was it because of my parents' tragedy, three generations of wasted lives, that I was unable to read novels or poetry? In my bookshop there would only be detective stories and books on religion, history and travel.)

Marika visited me, sometimes twice a month, proudly presenting her retirement card at the door, as Head of the Archives from the Bank of Salonika. After a chat in a secluded kebab house we'd race to catch up with the latest detective film. On winter nights, when those back in the dormitory were cursing and blinding to keep themselves warm, I'd be reciting belated prayers for Marika, this disabled woman who'd fired my passion for reading.

Our literature teacher was a learned Tartar, God bless him! He worked in the secondhand book business at weekends, and arranged work for me at the Enderun Book Conservation Workshop on Huzur Street, noble Çamlıca's arterial road. In the middle of a lonely hill adorned with uncut stones, a willow tree still stood, perhaps a sole survivor of an earthquake. I was nervous at first, working in the basement of the building in the shadow of that magnificent tree.

Baki Kutay, highly regarded in the book world as a restorer of antiquarian books, was a retired marine colonel. He was white-haired, white-bearded and, like many craftsmen, a silent scholar. If I succeeded in a trial period with him I was to undertake an apprenticeship in Enderun until my compulsory military service. My master didn't inquire into my past and made no move to encourage an interest in his craft.

At first I was afraid of this manly ex-sailor who lived with his ill-bred daughter Hale on the second floor of an old wooden building left him by his mother. Hale resembled Princess Caroline of Monaco but had no right arm, probably from birth. On the top floor of the building smeared with pest-resistant paint lived his granddaughter Dalga, a high-school student, and his sly daughter-in-law Sıla. Naval Lieutenant Nazım, Sıla's husband, had been killed during military manoeuvres. Dalga's name (Wave) made me smile when I first heard it, but later it spoke to me of depth. She was one of those unhappy people who are nevertheless a source of love. This tall enterprising girl was surely sent into the world to play volleyball. As I was leaving for military service she asked, God forgive me, 'Bedo, how old must men be before high-school girls can fall in love with them?'

The spacious first-floor drawing room had the atmosphere of a minimalist studio, despite the posters in Arabic script on the walls. My master worked reverently accompanied by instrumental music. He concentrated as though performing a life-or-death operation on these rare books, conversing, even flirting with them from time to time. The works he decided to save were given a dossier number, then restored, photographed and put away. If his clients were lost in admiration he was pleased but compliments annoyed him. For every hour spent on restoration he charged a fee of $50, adding fifty per cent for the materials he used. Clients from Europe and America, knowing there was no question of bargaining, were wary of arguing with him.

I didn't blame him for not trying to teach me his craft. For the apprentice secondhand bookseller 'book conservation' didn't always lead to the book trade and he was pleased to welcome any routine work I managed to handle. I respected my master Baki's pride and his genuine talent for eloquence and was glad he found no fault with my passion for detective stories.

'After the Holy Bible and the Koran, the most intelligent and worthwhile books are detective novels. The particular characteristic of the Holy Books is their immunity to misinterpretation. So many literary types owe their style to them,' he would say.

With my first wages I immediately acquired a Koran, a Bible and a Pentateuch. Compared with the others I found the Koran, the last to be written, the most compassionate and tolerant. Respectfully, I limited myself to reading it line by line. I found that when my eyes recited the music of the sentences, peace and calm embraced my soul. Every reading meant the discovery of new spiritual strength. Absorbing it did not change my attitude but perhaps my self-confidence increased. I was determined to come to terms with myself but I couldn't shake off my loneliness. I found a place for my own religion beyond that of the intellectuals and the religion-mongers, and I was attached to it by the coordinates of personal respect and love.

In the dark room next to the drawing room was a bookcase containing 2,000 handwritten rare and ancient manuscripts. I loved to breathe in the aroma of the manuscripts, none less than 250 years old. In my lino-floored bedroom between the Anatolian toilet and the library I read continuously, and on the evenings when my master was yelling at his daughter or daughter-in-law, I managed to avoid being dragged back to my rotten past by reciting Evliya Çelebi, the Ottoman travel writer.

Under his influence, and thanks to my education, physical size and increased self-confidence, I decided to do my military service as a commando. In mountainous Hakkâri I completed my service successfully, thank God, ending up with the rank of sergeant. I mustn't go into the military details. A commando shouldn't boast just because he's doing his duty! Towards the end of my military service I received two sad letters. Because of a neglected hernia Baki Kutay could no longer use his right hand and had finished with book conservation. And Marika, whom I loved much more than my father, had died.

With the help of a letter of recommendation from my company commander, God bless him, I got a day job in a security firm as soon as I returned to Istanbul. The firm had transformed a crude four-storey building in the modest district of Aksaray into a dormitory for unmarried workmen. After those action-packed days in Hakkâri, I grew bored with keeping watch at the door of a business office.

I bought scented Turkish Delight and went to kiss Baki Kutay's hand, but I noticed that my visit made him uncomfortable. He was drinking cognac and rereading *The Secret History of the Mongols*. I remember him saying, 'We are living more comfortably now that I'm gradually selling off my books. But what makes me sad is that all the old important works are taking refuge in foreign collections.'

Every family member was well; Dalga was at school. Baki's look intimated that I should go and not visit him again. As he said goodbye he addressed me by name for the first time. 'Hey, Bedirhan!', he said, 'being a commando seems to have done you good.'

∝

I headed for Tarlabaşı one last time to locate Marika's grave. A few steps beyond the main street that November morning I found myself travelling back in time. It was as if the labyrinthine street theatre I had left behind some 4,000 days before had been waiting for this moment to start again – the overhanging laundry that shields the sky, half-naked children playing football with empty plastic bottles, lazy granddads strolling around in every season in the same cardigans, restless youths dashing to the coffee houses to play board games till closing time, barber-shops, experts in alopecia, the dried-fruit shop with a sideline in faxes, and the pedlar of old clothes and birds, the abandoned Greek mansions with piles of waste on the street, despite the signs, 'Whoever dumps garbage here is a donkey,' posters from previous elections of well-groomed local candidates alongside leaflets by practitioners of circumcision pinned up by hand on wooden doors darkened by time, pithy notes written in chalk for workers come to read the electricity or water meters, near-illiterate praise for the Diyarbakırspor football team inscribed on walls that have once again resisted that final demolition order, young girls letting off steam as they brusquely sweep the narrow streets leading off the main thoroughfare – all these were not scenes I wanted to see.

The plague of rot that, despite nature and urban man, had failed to corrode the worn buildings within, had nevertheless inundated the streets. My nostrils became clogged with dirt as I climbed Paşa Bakkal Street. I walked up the stairs of the building with '1894' inscribed over the doorway, expecting to feel the whole street tremble. Semiha, who had been my mother and Marika's friend, was sitting there knitting away furiously.

My blood ran cold when I heard what she had to tell me.

Zazo, a drug addict gang leader, had broken into Marika's home, where he had strangled and raped her. Apparently he was still at large, and nobody had blown the whistle, obeying some principle of thieves' honour. I thought that life-and-death decisions taken in the blink of an eye belonged only in detective novels. But the moment

I got my breath back, I made up my mind that I would avenge Marika's death, assured that the people who hadn't informed on this creep certainly wouldn't inform on me.

My request for five-day leave was approved, and I was as delighted as a young artist granted time to complete a first commission. I learned that Zazo and two of his mates had taken over a building left empty due to an inheritance dispute. While the ground floor of the building with the ornate façade on Taksim Fırın Street was being used to store the loot, his two accomplices occupied the middle floor, and gang leader Zazo resided on the top floor. This experienced leader who delivered drugs to high schools was also involved in theft, and was a low-life pederast.

The gang members hung out at Dallas Teahouse on Turan Street, where vendors of music cassettes competed for trade through loudspeakers. The key to their house was left in an unlocked box at the main entrance for the use of friends, but was removed at night. One evening when the gang was intent on gambling, I borrowed the makeshift key to have a copy made, and asked a stammering street urchin, proud of his Werder Bremen shirt, to perform his good deed for the day by returning the key.

I stayed away for the next forty-eight hours.

On Saturday at midnight, with God's permission, I intended to raid the gang's headquarters. I could catch them off guard when they were flying high on hash after a rakı party.

Before slipping on my snow mask, in God's name, I

exchanged farewells and forgiveness with the Walther P–88 handgun. Amidst the squealing of mice I passed through the entrance, up to the middle floor, and approached the open door through which hoarse moans filtered. Zazo's two henchmen lay semiconscious as they watched a porn film in the living room. Suddenly my stomach turned, and I sent two bullets each into the heads of those lost young men.

I climbed the stairs, tiptoeing, determined. In my left hand Walther, its barrel growing nervous, in my right a torch. I inhaled the rosemary-scented aroma of the barrel of my pistol. Long live communal living, the upstairs door was open too! As the moans from the dimly-lit room increased my hands began to shake. I slowly peeped inside, where a tender young curly-haired boy lay on a bed, knocked out and probably doped by paint thinner. His naked body looked like a bag of bones. Zazo hadn't yet taken off his dirty underpants. He was like a vulture sniffing its victim, God forgive me!

I pointed the pistol at the bed, from three metres away, and screamed, 'Enough! You inhuman bastard!'

Astonished, Zazo slowly turned. There was a knife wound on the right side of his young, handsome face. Squinting his green eyes, he said, 'Who are you? What the hell do you want?' as he struggled to get the upper hand.

'I'm your Angel of Death, and I'm sending you to hell …'

As he reached for his knife under the pillow with

his left hand, I shot the first bullet into the middle of his forehead. Then into his mouth, and ear-holes! Your humble servant then lost his head, and with the red flick-knife of this compulsive criminal, he cut off his balls and penis. After stuffing his balls into his mouth and the other organ into the appropriate orifice, to set an example, I slipped down to the quiet street with a sense of relief and, in a south-eastern Turkish accent, called the police from a phone-box on Tarlabaşı Street, thinking that at least I'd given that poor young boy a second chance.

Then I stole away to the Unkapanı Bridge behind the Pera Palas Hotel. Some people had already entrusted their fishing-lines to the waters of the Golden Horn and were waiting idly. I felt as uneasy as if I'd gotten off at the wrong bus stop amidst this crowd of fishermen. Twenty steps away from the last amateur fisherman, whose eyes were fixed on the dark waters, I dropped the knife and pistol into the silence of the Golden Horn, in God's name.

Where the well-behaved Walther touched the surface, the water gleamed and was transformed into an almost infinite chain of circles.

I thought of how I'd set Marika's soul free from suffering, and how her frail eighty-year-old body had been touched by a man for the first time after her death. (I'm proud to say I have never laid a finger on a woman's body and have never masturbated except accidentally in sleep. I protect my self-respect from orgasms.)

Below Byzantium's Pantokrator Church, that stubborn

survivor, I got into a taxi reeking of cigarettes and sweat, and headed for Aksaray. The moustachioed folk-song-killer on the radio was bellowing, *If you meet with death / I'll be consumed with longing*. It must have been nerves, God forgive me, but I remember laughing to myself!

A

The chorus of 3,000 mosques reciting the afternoon ezan ended, and a mysterious impulse led me to my father's room, which I had seldom entered in the past. Now, after his death, I was free to come and go as I pleased. The uncomfortable thought that I might upset my mother, who buried the loss of her husband deep in her heart, lasted until her death.

İfakat had said of the gloomy room, 'Only a president would have a larger room than this.' In the only corner of the room not occupied by books there was a colossal TV set facing a burgundy-coloured leather armchair. From here my father would busy himself talking in numbers, solving equations, even as he watched documentaries or cartoons. Across from his desk, surrounded by a library of 20,000 books, was a conical aquarium. I knew that this glass environment, with its dozen playful, colourful fish, would be destroyed after my father's death.

My father was the son of an officer with roots in Kırklareli who, the very month he was promoted to captain in the gendarmerie, was treacherously killed on the south-east frontier by a smuggler. My father's widowed mother married her cousin, and he was left to be brought up by his aunt. She was a teacher of Turkish, who never married after her fiancé drowned at the Florya beach. (According to İfakat, my mother had always mistreated his aunt, who died of grief.)

He graduated with top grades from Darüşşafaka High School (selected by an exam for orphans), won a bursary to Berkeley, studied mathematics, and remained there until he became a professor. He never returned to America after he was summoned by his aunt to get married in Istanbul.

Don't assume I was always under my mother's thumb. It seems I was a hyperactive child. Caressing me affectionately, my father would call me 'Squirrel', and if he took an interest in me, I would be as delighted as if I had been praised at school. I couldn't decide if I was being allowed to share his trips to unmapped slum neighbourhoods or to forgotten Byzantine and Ottoman monuments as a kind of reward. I hesitated to ask the reason for his passion and I felt embarrassed as I watched him caressing and whispering to old stone Ottoman basins. When spring came to Çamlıca, I recall hopping off the narrow pavements and walking down the street that passed by our mansion to the market square, till we eventually reached the last mansion on Alemdağ Street. If he walked ahead, hands behind his back, I'd run after him in a panic.

I have always accepted the quiet nature of Çamlıca's slopes, forgotten in the time tunnel of the last forty years. The visual resistance to time lingers on in several dwellings, and in their gardens, visible beyond tired old walls and abandoned mansions where remnants of chimneys or thresholds still survive. Life goes on as usual in these mansions, behind closed, lace curtains, and in gardens without the sound of children's voices. I would watch the drama of the local residents in their drab outfits, appearing suddenly in the deserted main road from nameless side streets.

The market consisted of two-storey miniature shops at the crossroads.

'There's no smaller market', said my father, 'even in the exile towns of Anatolia.'

He liked the claustrophobic stationery shop opposite the Çamlıca Sports Headquarters, which acted as a licensed Lotto outlet and newspaper distributor, and dealt in PVC coating and dry-cleaning. The polite owner would timidly watch the Hodja studying the numerical distribution of the Lotto coupons. On our last visit, my father pointed at the tax plate hung next to the window and giggled, 'Did you know this shop pays more tax than your grandfather, Squirrel?'

If Vecihi, the veteran calligrapher with the prosthetic

arm, was back from the mosque, we would drop by his derelict shop in Kısıklı Street. My father knew this white-bearded man was from Giresun, in the Black Sea region, but he called him fellow townsman, and if Vecihi was in a bad mood, he would sit him down to play backgammon and, just to console him, defeat him by just one game, 5–4.

There would also be uproarious backgammon sessions with his bibliophile student, Cemail, his mate and confidant from high-school days, now retired as personnel director of a foreign pharmaceutical firm, but who had not yet given up his wooden house in modest Eyüp. With my own eyes I saw him play chess with the ventriloquist, who never revealed in which mosque he worked as muezzin, and with the *çiğ köfte*[1] chef, who had two wives.

The banker Selçuk Altun, the son of a retired governor who was my father's childhood friend, was allowed to go in and out of his room whenever he wished. My mother had accepted this temperamental bibliomaniac who was the same age as herself. I was never happy to see this unattractive man in our house. His three novels were published after my father's death, and I sensed that one day he would exploit our secret drama, exposing it in one of his books.

My father played the *ney*[2] in private, and played it well. Sometimes twice a week, he would embrace his silver-ringed instrument, reverently tilting his head to the left.

---

1   A meat rissole eaten raw.
2   A reed flute used in Mevlevi music.

Hiding by the door, I would hear the enchanted tunes he blew, and close my eyes in pleasure. During my journeys in the time tunnel, the deep sounds of the ezan and the smells of sesame pitta accompanied my pauses by tombs, fountains and mosque courtyards. If spring was over and the lazy balcony door left open, I feared that our garden would be invaded by silly kids, seduced by the magical music, just as in *The Pied Piper of Hamelin*. I recall our last conversation, and how I thought of becoming a guitarist when I grew up. He had said, 'Become one, Squirrel, if you can make your instrument talk like Mark Knopfler.' But when I entered my mother's august presence to ask her permission, she said, 'You will know what you're going to be when you reach high school. But I can assure you, Arda, that your becoming a flea-ridden musician does not figure in my plans right now.'

☙

My father, as well as being able to remember his identity, retirement, passport and credit card numbers, was a treasure-house of general knowledge. Early on he had noticed my stubborn refusal to enter the gravitational field of mathematics, but he would thank 'Graph Theory' for his own stock of knowledge. I am aware that it wouldn't be satisfactory to summarize Graph Theory as 'the ability to define the concepts of daily life that relate to mathematics, in the language of numbers'. (Maybe it would be more enlightening to give you the crazy example of how to take a mouse, a cat and a snake, all alive, across a river, using two rowboats, and pull this concept to shreds by mathematics.)

Thanks to his search for signs of his 'divine concept' in the grouping structure of aquarium fish or migrant birds in motion, or in the order of distribution of exits in a stadium, I gave up mathematics quite early on.

After retirement he wrote courageous essays in leading newspapers and magazines on serious topics: the shallowness of society, bad design in urban expansion, religious exploitation, public health, educational and cultural crises. Several controversial essays appeared in *Turkey Should Not Be Proud of Me*, his book of collected writings – 'P. Mondrian: Murderer of Modern Painting', 'The Greatest Novelist on The Planet: John Fowles', 'The Only Philosopher to be Taken Seriously: Anti-Philosopher, Ludwig Wittgenstein', were some of the titles I admired.

In his well-known essay, 'Shantytown Man: The Rebel Shaped by Poverty', he emphasized the fact that the same people who took over public property and used illegal electricity and water had also taken over the running of local government. According to him, the class that continued to grow in a superficial environment of frivolity and intimidation would, in ten years' time, start to produce ministers and prime ministers.

He was a regular participant in interviews and television panels and always attacked those fundamentalist columnists and members of parliament in particular.

The name of the terrorist organization El Mekrub[1] was first heard when they murdered my father as we were waiting for him to turn up at my fourteenth birthday party.

_____

[1]   In Arabic, 'The Concerned' / 'The Caring'.

B

According to Enes, when Our Lord the Prophet set out for the Holy War, he announced:
'My Lord God! You are my help and support. Thanks to you, we will think of remedies, thanks to you, we will attack, and thanks to you, we will do battle.'

Tirmizi

Even when I'm on leave from my humiliating work I view the minimum-wage earners scurrying in all directions with amazement.

My introduction to the psychopath, Baybora, occurred when I was taking a day off work. I was walking along Çadırcılar Street, heading for the Özlem Meat Restaurant, in a state of aimless contentment. (After dinner I was going to buy a book about Immortal Hızır from the

Sahaflar book-market and then go to the cinema.) In Çadırcılar, where the dearest article of clothing is $15, the Moldavian girls must still be using their body language to bargain with shopkeepers. Once again I caught all those sex-starved men in the area stripping them with their eyes. I think that the pleasure I derive from reading Evliya Çelebi is comparable to the basic human sex drive.

My favourite soup kitchen is by the Lütfullah Gate in the left wing of the Grand Bazaar. Over the arched entrance is engraved the year when space was allotted for more than 4,400 shops. I was upset at being unable to subtract 1461 from 1991 to figure out its age. I can send a bullet through the eye of a needle while at the same time dealing with a couple of roughnecks, but I've no head for mathematics. As a result I'd shied away from the secondhand book business.

Coming out of the soup kitchen, and struggling with a broken toothpick in my mouth, I was addressed by a stout man with a face like a self-satisfied turkey.

'I hope you enjoyed your meal, Commando Bedirhan!' he said. With his bureaucrat's air, this fifty-year-old pain in the neck was grabbing the opportunity to thrust his forged business card under my nose: 'Ali Hadi Bora – Retired Chief Inspector'. I was taken aback when he continued, 'Don't worry, Commando. If you just listen to me for ten minutes, I have a terrific offer for you.' Taking my arm, he pushed me into the first empty coffee house, and took it upon himself to order two sage teas.

'You did good work in Tarlabaşı, congratulations! Because you handed out retribution to those killer-robots, prayers for you will never cease. Your dossier is reckoned to be closed. According to the tabloids, "The rival gangs have settled old scores." Because of insensitivity, fear, the legal vacuum and bureaucracy, in Istanbul particularly, so many hoodlums like Zazo who've damaged the social order are obstructing the state's good works.

'To be frank, I'm a member of an organization called Mecruh, whose dream is to eliminate microbes like him. *Mecruh* means "hurt" or "injured" in Arabic. In exchange for a fee from injured clients we assist justice by restoring their rights. We are incredibly powerful, consisting of élite members. If you join as our hitman, you will achieve material and spiritual prosperity. You will usually be required to do one job a year, and your salary will begin at $100,000, with a down payment of 20 per cent. If all goes well, you'll be a millionaire in ten years. Let me add, while I remember, that Mecruh never sheds any innocent blood for money.

'You are strong, a true marksman, you keep your mouth shut, you don't chase after sex and you're on your own. Commando, you must have been sent from heaven to do this work. I'll balance your passion for books with personal training. (If you join us I'll be your contact.) We will never use the Tarlabaşı incident against you. But if we wish, we can get rid of you for crimes you've never even committed, my dear veteran of Hakkâri.

'We offer you a job which is well paid, exciting and

beneficial to society. There's $5,000 in the envelope I'm putting in your pocket. Consider it a gift. You'll be on leave on Thursday next week. We can meet then at the same time in this pissy coffee house. Think about it. If you don't come back here in seven days, the money in your pocket is as much yours as your mother's white milk.

'I know you're about to buy a book from the secondhand book-market and then rush off to the Şafak Cinema in Çemberlitaş. But don't forget, Commando, there are pleasures more profound.'

∞

I insisted on two things: the hideous, grotesque Baybora must persuade me of the victim's guilt and must never again address me as 'Commando' in his insolent way.

My first job was to punish a professor of mathematics, a pretentious follower of the West who insulted our religion in his speech and writings, and cheated on his wife, the Jewish convert to Islam, whose money funded his opulent lifestyle. (The dossier prepared by the organization included – as if it were necessary – his ability to multiply five-digit numbers in his head with the speed of a computer.) In the photographs taken secretly for the dossier, the professor's attitude to other people seemed rude and belittling. If he had asked me at any time to solve an arithmetic problem, I would have been ashamed and embarrassed. My trigger finger began to twitch.

I was going to lay an ambush for him in a lonely street

in Üsküdar where, God forgive him, he used to meet his lover. Baybora, for the first and last time, had poked his crow's beak into this business on the pretext of assisting my training. Respectfully, I passed the endless walls of the Karacaahmet Cemetery till I reached shady Eşrefsaat Street. It seemed that in pursuit of his intrigues, at 3 o'clock on Tuesdays and Saturdays, the immoral professor would turn from Rumi Paşa Mosque into neighbouring Çeşme-i Cedit Street. Before my reconnaissance expeditions into a district which had still preserved its sacred Ottoman origins, including even street names, I had taken ten days' leave without pay, and step by step I had traced the journey of the wretched 60-year-old to his love nest. The vulgar womanizer would swagger along, and I was sure that as he got out of the taxi he never even raised his head to glance at the elegant 500-year-old mosque opposite. I couldn't help wondering how much daily profit a Çadırcılar trader would need to make to buy his cap with the earflaps, his leather jacket and suede boots.

In the mosque courtyard I patiently traced, stone by stone, the geometrical tomb of Rumi Mehmet Paşa, Grand Vizier from 1466 to 1469. Clumps of couch grass had invaded the slope of the family tombs. But between the sunken mosque walls and the cornerstones of the street the sloping building site seemed more level. A vigorous blanket of mallow-like weeds spread 150 metres around the young plantation. The space between the mosque wall and the neglected building to the east of the site, which autumn rains had turned into a sea of mud, was separated by a barbed-wire fence. I'm indebted to the heroic street cats for the idea of climbing over that rusty fence two metres high to the street below.

Forty minutes beforehand, I hid my grey cap and false beard in a nook to the right of the fence. I was concentrating on *The Syriacs in History* when the victim's taxi arrived. He deigned to get out of the shabby vehicle, muttering at the poor driver. Scrutinizing both ends of the deserted street I leapt into the bushes. Between us was a space of perhaps thirty metres. I drew Walther II, in the name of God, while the professor was putting on his hat, and fired six bullets into the chest and heart of the man who could multiply five-digit numbers in his head. Leaping over the wire fence, I landed first in neighbouring Parlak Street, then ran on into Şemsi Paşa Road. I jumped into an old taxi heading for the Unkapanı Bridge with 'Old Chap, Business is Crap' written on the back window. At the spot where I'd chucked away Walther I, I committed Walther II to the blessed protection of the Golden Horn. Baybora had warned me, 'Don't look at the newspapers for two weeks.' While I was failing mentally to convert into Turkish lira the $150,000 I would earn in exchange for those six bullets, I had come to the Valens Aqueduct erected in AD 373. Was it nerves? God forgive me, I remember I began to laugh ...

A

A pleasant autumn was approaching. As the evening ezan rose from mosque to mosque I stood up from the desk and went out onto the balcony. I don't know a more strategic point from which to observe the monumental trees. Beyond the field of red and white tulips that surrounds the pool begins the display of cedar, pistachio and chestnut trees and oleanders. The family's favourite plant was the absurd Japanese persimmon that sheltered under the wall. My father praised the apple-like fruit of the tree that loses its symmetrical leaves before winter. As the orange fruit of the bare plant gleamed in the dusk he would declare, 'This is the painting by Nature that defeated René Magritte.'

As the ezan died away, the wind began to wander here and there. I was sheltering in the room where I could sit back comfortably at my father's desk. For the first time

I noticed the pencil case of Armenian silverwork in the middle of the bulky wooden desk. Beside it was the bronze statue of Eros, a span high, which my mother, searching for a present for my father's sixtieth birthday, had asked Selçuk Altun to buy at a Sotheby's auction. It seemed I had failed to notice the sorrowful face of the naked object. Authentic icons were scattered throughout spaces on the bookshelves – silver vases made in Iran, a miniature yacht in a bottle, knick-knacks of half-naked naiads, grotesque porcelain figures, a giant bee imprisoned in an amber egg, three dried seahorses and a ruby globe scattering flaming light onto the shelf of dictionaries. As a first-time museum addict I would examine the date (19 June 1990) of the fall of the Berlin wall, and a heap of rubble, including early Byzantine coins. On a shelf containing the works of Aulus Gellius stood a glass cube engraved with one of Ludwig Wittgenstein's aphorisms. And above the science volumes, on a shelf that included a handwritten fifteenth-century work on geometry, a young shark, three and a half spans in length, stuffed with cotton, was waiting patiently, open-mouthed.

In the drawing room, before starting on the first bottle in the drinks cabinet, I made a quick, guilty search of the desk drawers. In the lower left drawer lay a forgotten copy of *A King's Story*, the autobiography of King Edward VIII, who abdicated in order to wed an American widow. Inside the front cover I caught sight of the cassette of a work by Dvořák, my father's favourite composer. Beneath

'Songs My Mother Taught Me', the fourth section of Op. 55 – the *Gypsy Melodies* – were pencilled three question marks. (Suppose I hadn't been curious about the bulge in the book?) The colour photograph, postcard size, which fell to the floor had been taken under an arbour on my ninth birthday. On either side of my father, Dalga and I were putting on a smile for my mother's camera. I was shaken by painful feelings and quickly shrugged off the effect of the alcohol that had failed to anaesthetize my body. I imagined the tired pine needles flying skywards in a disciplined formation, and travelled back in hope to twenty years ago. Stroking the wings of Eros, I whispered Bufalino's poetic aphorism, 'What sad days those were, the happiest of my life.'

◌

Until her breasts began to appear, Dalga and I used to wrestle, no holds barred, pushing and shoving and horsing around. Unfortunately she was four years older than me. When I was ten I realized we were physically different, and at eleven I fell hopelessly in love. If the ancient doorbell rang – two short rings, one long – for the swimming pool, I enjoyed an additional pleasure. When we were sunbathing together I would make an excuse to go to my room, where I would masturbate as I stared intently through field-glasses at every inch of her long plump legs and her strong round hips.

In our neighbourhood, her silent mother Sıla, whom

my mother called 'the Francophone with half a talent', was my mother's close friend and bridge partner. She had lost her naval-officer husband in an accident while he was on duty, and she and her daughter had taken refuge with her father-in-law. İfakat kept asking if the little Georgian beauty was taking an interest in the assistant head of the lyceé where she taught French, although he was married and younger than herself.

My father didn't like Dalga's churlish grandfather, who busied himself with the restoration of old books, and declared, 'The megalomaniac dotard's sweat stinks of glue and his soul of cellophane.' Her one-armed aunt Hale survived on tranquillizers accompanied by non-filter cigarettes, read long novels and wept copiously. It was five minutes' walk to our mansion and they were content that we didn't often visit their haunted house.

'Dalga, take care not to let go of Arda's hand.' Of all my mother's orders, that was my favourite. We would go together hand-in-hand to the film or play or concert she had chosen. As Dalga's long slender fingers touched mine my heart trembled and flew off in a series of fantasies. Even though we were inseparable for six years, I gradually got fed up with people who thought we were brother and sister.

She would pull my hair like an older sister and declare, 'I can't imagine any girl who wouldn't shag you for those blue eyes,' and I'd scan her charming face in a panic. When I stammered out that she looked like Cleopatra with her snow-white skin, her deep dark eyes, upturned nose and smooth hair, she would say, 'Sod off!'

I knew that when she completed her education at the American High School at Üsküdar I would be at a loss. In her second year of school she was captain of the girls' volleyball team, but when she was suddenly transferred to Fenerbahçe, I immediately became a Fenerbahçe fan. I went with Hayrullah our chauffeur to every match played by the Fenerbahçe Women's Team. Sometimes my father joined us. He liked Dalga and sometimes helped her with her homework. I would pray silently all through the match and if Dalga made a strategic mistake I'd be on the verge of tears. The stress I felt when she had the ball, and all the spectators stared at her legs and hips, continued even after the match.

'Couldn't my mother arrange to send Dalga to matches in a tracksuit?' I asked, and my father would laugh scornfully.

I was always praying that the water would be cut off in Dalga's house. Then she'd come and bathe in my personal bathroom. (My mother had had panes of glass fitted in two upper corners of the lavatory door – she wanted to keep an eye on me even *there*.) As soon as I heard the sound of water, I would stand on a wobbly chair and glue my eyes to the door, tracing every inch of her naked body. İfakat knew that I was aware of her own secret relationship with Hayrullah, and when she caught me at it she'd giggle, 'If you fell and broke a bone you couldn't even cry.'

Once while we were watching a romantic film on video together, Dalga said, 'I'm in no hurry to fall in love, but if I ever meet the perfect man you'll be the first to know,' and my heart sank. After this declaration I was deeply depressed. (If she came one day and whispered in my ear the name of some volleyball player, and I didn't die of a heart attack, then I'd kill myself.) Maybe if I did everything my mother asked, Eros the Angel of Love would save Dalga from the perfect man and award the prize to me ... My accomplice İfakat advised, 'When you begin university the age difference between you will get less.' When my height reached 1.77 metres I could admit proudly that I'd loved her since I was ten ...

In her last year at the American High School, Dalga and her mother left Çamlıca without telling anyone. My mother said, 'Sıla had big problems with her father-in-law. They'll visit us as soon as they've settled down.' But before we had time to miss Dalga, we lost my father. Without a goodbye, Dalga's grandfather and aunt also departed and I knew I would hear little from my mother when I enquired about her again.

I never fell in love again after Dalga. Being in my mother's shadow it wasn't necessary, because my mother did my thinking for me better than I did for myself.

෴

As the wind died down I went out onto the balcony to face the evening ezan. I watched the wind's querulous fight with the date-palms and its persistence in the star-protected sky. Bored, I focused on the cityscape on the other side. I tried to share my grief with the fading points of light that leaked from 10,000 dwellings. 'I wonder in which one Dalga is making love with the love of her life.' I had to shake myself free of my paranoia. Suddenly I had a brainwave. I decided on the attractive idea of not guessing what would happen next. Even though my height stuck at 1.75 metres, I would look for her. If necessary I would find her by pacing the streets of Istanbul. Thanks to sleeping pills, I had remained in bed for seventy-two hours in a lethargic stupor, and had even begun to hear Dalga's tantalizing voice. Whether she was laughing or crying was all the same to me.

B

According to the Venerable Omar, Our Lord the Prophet uttered the following sayings:
'When you come upon a sick man, ask him to pray for you. For his prayer is like the prayer of angels.'
Ibn-i Mace

God bless my first victim! With the money I had earned I decided to move to the tranquil district of Üsküdar, which I had come to know well through my explorations. The dignified Ottoman soul still pervaded streets with awe-inspiring names. When I saw those dry but elegantly carved fountains, the mottled tombs and the fine mosques built for pashas, my zest for life returned. Meeting an old lady resting at the top of a hill muttering prayers, I could ignore the screaming children in the historical garden now reduced to a wood depot. Modest young girls in headscarves coming out of these wooden buildings immediately lowered their eyes to street level. There were pious grocers still patiently persevering in lonely basement shops. I was pleased that no other space could be converted into a dull coffee house where idlers also gamble. On the easygoing streets with their commercial signs, people walked slowly and solemnly, while on the wider roads I observed retired bureaucrats washing their old cars with exaggerated ceremony.

In Ottoman Turkish, *tephir* means 'steaming'. When I saw the wooden house with its carved façade in Tephirhane Street, adjacent to Eşrefsaat, I repeated my favourite prayer three times and swore to give up my miserable work.

The estate agent told me, 'Rezzan Ergene will show you an apartment to rent: she's the granddaughter of an Ottoman pasha,' and my knees trembled. I knew that the landlady, who was over seventy, would give me the once-over. I remember climbing up the to the fourth floor, with great respect for the old polished staircase. Regal Rezzan whispered that the furnished apartment belonged to her son Gürsel, who had a psychological problem that had kept him in hospital a long time. His personal belongings were locked in a sparsely furnished room. A partly empty mahogany bookcase in the sitting room was, of course, of special interest to your humble servant. I found myself almost blessing Baybora for helping me to acquire a place of my own for the first time in my life. When Rezzan, in her comical make-up, heard I could pay six months' rent in advance, she began to address yours truly as, 'Bedirhan, my dear man'. And when the estate agent realized I didn't want a receipt for his commission he plied me with advance information about the Ergene family.

'Rezzan is on the floor beneath you. She lives with her daughter Emel, the divorcée. She sometimes works in one of those palaces turned museums. When Rezzan's late husband first entered the Ergene family he was given the family name. This lawyer, who died the day the ruling political party was established, managed to be a member of the Turkish Parliament for two consecutive terms, one year on the left, one on the right.

'Throughout history this parasitic family has first exploited the Ottomans, and now our Republic. Twenty years ago they sold their summer homes in prestigious Salacak and made a forced landing in our neighbourhood. I don't think any of their properties remain, except a dilapidated workshop at historical Sultanhamam and this building. Gürsel, a prominent member of the family, was studying philosophy in the US when his mother made him come back to Turkey and he fell into a depression. The poor, honest gentleman is three years younger than Emel, who's in her fifties, and for the last two years has been having treatment at La Paix Hospital. When Rezzan moved here from Salacak, she made every minute hell for the family she controls.

'Her brother Renan, who has looked about fifty for the

last twenty years, lives on the second floor. A confirmed bachelor, he came into the world to make fun of it. He went to university in Paris and returned five years later, still a second-year student and, having done almost no work, somehow managed to retire. He is perpetually annoyed with his elder sister. He imagines he's a talented harlequin and magician. He has made the ground floor into a studio for repairing stringed instruments but it has become a central meeting-place for down-and-out gamblers.

'You seem like a suitable young man. If you pay your rent regularly and steer clear of the Ergenes you'll be all right. They're eccentric people, but with aristocratic manners.'

The poncy estate agent seemed put out when he saw I wasn't alarmed by his tirade. But I had certainly warmed to my neighbours, who I hoped wouldn't disturb my privacy.

☙

I confess that when I registered for a British Council language course in İstiklal Street, it was really just to read the great thriller writers like Raymond Chandler, Dashiell Hammett and Patricia Highsmith in the original. But I couldn't get to like noisy İstiklâl Street or the motley crowd on the course who'd joined only to chase after promotion or to find a mate. They laughed at my pronunciation of the word 'cafeteria'. (But permit your humble servant to inform you that he got the highest grades in his written exams.)

Guided by my mentor, who was himself addicted to thrillers, I was destined to become acquainted with the works of many good writers, including Georges Simenon, Eric Ambler, Graham Greene and Cornell Woolrich.

I was going to be working three times a week at a secondhand bookshop called Zarathustra. Sami Sakallı, associate professor of literature who was chucked out of the university for his left-wing views, wise bookseller, author, editor and translator, had said, 'Whenever you want, there is work for you here in this poor little shop.' I would have accepted the minimum wage so as not to offend him. My master was known as 'Nietzsche' because of his fierce facial expressions and I am sure he was quite pleased when I rose to greet him when he entered the shop. I soon grew accustomed to the small secondhand book business with its narrow interests. On Saturdays, when Sami took part in absurd polemics with his turncoat fellow-travellers, he emerged as a humane man of principle. I was proud of the fact that we were one of the rare bookshops in the market that didn't resort to selling secondhand school textbooks when business was slack. Due to my master's illness and family problems, I pretty much ran the shop on my own, completing my own library by buying books above the market price. But before three years were up I'd abandoned the struggle to keep this unrewarding job, which I had thought ideal for me. I just couldn't handle the financial side of things.

His ideological and financial problems, his superficial

wife and vagabond son, his smoking and drinking, all conspired to give my master cancer. After his death, his ungrateful son, Kuzey, is said to have sold the 7,000 books in Zarathustra's by the kilo, in order to pay off his debts to a moneylender.

In Ahmed Hamdi Tanpınar's masterpiece, *Five Cities*, he introduces the Istanbul of previous centuries as 'a city of great works of architecture, of little corners and surprise landscapes. In these, the heart of Istanbul is to be found.' On Sundays I used to visit the monuments that were still extant, in those 'little corners and surprise landscapes' that had the luck to survive in the suburbs of Istanbul. I would compose prayers as I traced them, stone by stone, and wished for patience with a humanity that was useless as bird droppings.

ରେ

I knew that within the month Rezzan would visit my place to see I hadn't turned it into a tip, and that she'd be touched when she heard I was following an English language course while working in the secondhand book-market. It was a clear sign of her good breeding that she never queried my story of the rich parents I'd lost in a traffic accident.

'Where on earth, my dear, did you get the idea of wearing a brown shirt with blue jeans?' she asked, and my heart warmed to her. We took to making monthly visits to local theatres full of swarthy humanity, and twice to the supermarket Migros. She announced when it was time to get new clothes and didn't hesitate to choose them for me. I would be roused from sleep or a meal by that voice of hers, made both to give orders and polite requests, and sent out to find her favourite Ottoman pudding or drink. (I could never refuse or ask her to pay for her orders.) If she quarrelled with her daughter, I could be immediately summoned below. Muttering a formal prayer, I'd enter the high-ceilinged, historic house, but I didn't dare set foot on the silk carpet in her drawing room. The five splendid Ottoman landscapes on the walls were by our famous painter, Hodja Ali Rıza. My heart broke when she spoke of the pictures I gazed at so respectfully.

'My child, I've nothing more to sell but my soul.'

Looking through an album of faded photographs, I hoped to hear more of her full life, but instead I heard only complaints about how she'd always been misunderstood. She told me of her dreams, while drinking black coffee and smoking cigarettes, and gossiped about her bridge partners. She insisted she felt no sadness, except for the academic son she had abandoned in a corner of a murky hospital, and for the loss of her maternal pride.

I had to sort out my relationship with Emel and Renan, whom I had chosen to ignore. One night, after a trip to Lakeside Abant with her mother's quartet of bridge players, the drunk Emel, glass in hand, pounded on my door shouting, 'I've come to see if your tool matches your height.' When she ignored my warning and tried to walk in, I slapped her twice. I think she ran home in tears, almost sober. I knew she wouldn't be able to look me in the eye when we met again. As for me, the fingertips of my right hand would tingle with embarrassment.

Renan never stopped teasing me. When he wasn't doing animal impressions, he was uttering offensive Kurdish-sounding words behind my back. One Saturday morning while heading for Zarathustra I went down to the front door, where he was exchanging racing tips with two other lazy fellows. He returned my desultory greeting by identifying your humble servant as a terrorist, and I flipped. Approaching in God's name, I started to squeeze his big nose with my index and middle fingers. I knew he would act like a cartoon character and start cackling like a hen.

'What do you think you're doing, you ignorant peasant from the mountains?'

I squeezed tighter after every sentence, till he said, 'Don't you know that I work with the Secret Service? You don't realize how many generals I know! Are you a pervert or what? Look, I'm begging you …'

He was sweating profusely and snot was running down his red nose. Eventually I tossed the quivering, helpless man to the ground as he pleaded, 'Don't hurt me, I'll eat your shit.' But I hadn't got over my rage; I landed a couple of heavy Ottoman blows on each of the young idlers as, stupefied, they watched the poor old man whose home and money they had freely abused. Then I rushed out into peaceful Şemsi Paşa Avenue, satisfied.

ॐ

To make sure I was still under his thumb, Baybora would ring me once a month with a series of questions like, 'Are you going regularly to the shooting range to practise? Are you keeping more than $20,000 in the bank?'

One day during the holy Kurban festival, fate brought us together at the Kanaat Lokanta Restaurant. I knew I was to be given notice of a second commission. A plastic file with a foreign brand name was squeezed into my hand under the table and my heart sank. If the Organization had deliberately chosen the postcard-sized photograph on the first page to annoy me, they were to be congratulated. I was nauseated by the unpleasant image of a thirty-year-old man with his thin, pointed moustache, grinning maliciously at his prey. Why does the Anatolian male insist on the moustache habit? If it is a symbol of manhood, why is it forbidden in the army and the police force? Whenever a disastrous crisis erupts in our country, there's always someone with an ugly moustache involved.

Hamit Özay, son-in-law to Hadji Mümin Cömert, the manufacturer of cotton thread. God knows how many million dollars he blackmailed Cömert into paying. (A gambling debt and a sexual addiction had brought him into the clutches of a debt-collector's gang.) If he couldn't get what he wanted, he had sworn to hand over evidence of illegal sales to the Department of Finance. They say that before the noon ezan he began to drown his sorrows in the rakı he hid in his room, a mischief-maker intended for the Ramadan fast …

I imagine Baybora intended this last sentence to have a powerful effect on me.

'Surely it doesn't suit our Holy Hadji not to give a receipt?' I asked.

'Ah, my naive warrior, it's a speciality of the industry that includes our Holy Hadji's business. If your rivals sell off the record and you can't, you'll soon sink. The main problem here is the failure of government to bring about any dynamic tax changes. I don't know what kind of books you're reading, but I do know that thirty per cent of our national income is unregistered.'

In practical terms, apart from his continuous bag of tricks, you couldn't find fault with babbling Baybora on this point. When I examined the dossier drawn up with Hadji's collaboration it was clear to me that I was to catch the louse Hamit in the act and punish him. For ten days I pursued the wastrel son-in-law. Twice a week a pimp who serviced the houses brought along a young girl or a transvestite to his bachelor flat in secluded Ataşehir, and three hours later he came back in a car and took away the poor exhausted creatures. While I was exploring the soulless modern district I finished His Excellency Ibn Battuta's *Seyahatname* (Book of Travels). (Between 1325 and 1354 he had travelled through several Islamic countries but was most impressed by those under Ottoman rule, and praised Alanya above all cities.) As I was reciting the last page of his masterpiece under my breath, I remember a huge transvestite emerging from the flat and throwing himself into the waiting minibus.

As the evening traffic in front of the building eased off, I broke in with the help of a master key that fitted the main door of the apartment block. No lift, so I climbed up to the ninth floor, disgusted by the staircase that reeked of fish and meat. Not a sound from inside as I fingered the key of the flat. I was shocked that the crude curses I heard from a neighbouring household came from a woman. The flat was furnished as bleakly as a hotel room and the sitting-room walls were a shameful display of transvestite posters. For one moment, God forgive me, I thought that some of the male figures in their make-up were more attractive than the female fashion models. The pervert son-in-law had passed out in his bedroom wearing nothing but his underwear.

Even in his sleep he didn't look innocent. I pumped a single bullet into his heart and pushed Walther III into his right hand. According to the instructions from Baybora it must look like a suicide. Otherwise yours truly would have woken the victim and given him the chance to draw his gun. On the vulgar commode I noted a book entitled *Türkiye Benimle Gurur Duymasın* (Turkey Should Not Be Proud of Me). 'Now Turkey won't even be ashamed of you,' I said and immediately regretted this stupid remark.

CR

With God's help, I successfully achieved all seventeen of my 'missions'. I never disposed of anyone as easily as the ungrateful son-in-law. Some wept and offered me bribes, some crouched at my feet or bit my hand, some spat in my face and drew a gun. I emptied my magazine into the belly of the last one. I almost faint when I recall the revolting stench of his intestines gushing out.

I counted every mission a sacred duty and was content to live a secret life of planning, spying, stalking and ambushing. I wasn't concerned with the way of life or speech of the appointed victims before their deaths. Did I find the moment when the bullet met the target, or when I smelled the tantalizing aroma of the gun-barrel, as stimulating as reading?

CR

Sami Sakallı's friend, Cemil Nejat İlker, God bless him, thought I might starve when Zarathustra closed, and so arranged a part-time job for me with an agency that published magazines for private corporations. When I heard that I would be working as assistant editor and proofreader, I was as proud as on the day when I was promoted to sergeant.

I waited till I'd finished the last lap of the English-language course I'd been patiently attending before rummaging through my predecessor's library. On the top shelf, among philosophy and psychology books, were some heavy documents, one of which I dropped on the floor. It was Gürsel Ergene's private notebook. This Venetian-bound volume revealed how he had finished his schooling at St Joseph's Lycée and gone to the US, what he suffered at university and later on. I read of his poetic anger at his disillusionment, his stubborn, shattered dreams of an honest world. And I was curious about a man who sought any excuse to hurt himself, and in particular his mother.

The following are extracts from the period that concluded with his banishment to a hospital, to be treated for his illness:

I wanted an academic career in the field of contemporary literature. I wanted to translate, to explore neglected writers and poets, to write essays and critical papers. When she failed to make her useless husband into a minister, my mother intended to make sure I would become a philosopher. Her command was absolute. I went to America to read philosophy and I was to return to Turkey when I had finished my doctorate …

Our fashionable philosopher of the moment was Wittgenstein, the anti-philosopher. Let's see if another such brilliant star will appear, finely balanced between genius and madness …

Finally my mother and I came to an agreement. I would return to Istanbul when I became an associate professor, and she would allow me to marry Betsy …

Betsy, an associate professor of social psychology, never cared for Istanbul, Üsküdar, or my mother, nor for the pittance she would earn for part-time jobs, or for the insensitivity of academics ...

After our engagement Betsy would say, 'I'll go to the ends of the earth with you,' but she despised the suburban Istanbul dweller who couldn't even carry a shopping basket in the supermarket. And, according to my mother, Betsy was happy to ignore the city's advantages and was flirting with a married banker whom she had met on her runs in Yıldız Park. When her suggestion of returning to California was rejected, divorce became inevitable ...

My older sister was jealous of my mother's interest in me during my childhood, and later, in her adolescence, of my academic success. Her suppressed feelings, developed over twenty-five years, revealed themselves under the influence of alcohol. If I'd had a bigger salary I'd have moved away long ago from this mouldy ruin of a city ...

On the eve of returning to Istanbul I had prepared myself for the very worst. I must have felt ashamed of my powers of imagination, which had underestimated the magnitude of 'the worst'; hyperinflation had turned a shallow leaderless country into a tribe of nomads. From the ashes of Constantinople, the great city that ignited the Renaissance, had risen a modern village haunted by ghosts of the past. Moustachioed peasants had seized control of the government. A mob ignorant of literature or art (there is no equivalent word for 'Philistine' in Turkish – a great pity!)

were indifferent to the rampant corruption. Academic life was strangled by a mass of insensitivities. My colleagues were bored and poor. They think that with my degree from Berkeley I'm crazy not to go abroad (or in the midst of chaos am I struggling to face a punishment I deserve?) …

The academic faculties are divided primarily into two factions, left and right: the time is surely coming when they'll unite to criticize me. My promotion is delayed and the article I wrote for the college magazine is irresponsibly censored. Sycophantic deans ignorant of any other language are sent abroad to symposia. Students turn up to class occasionally and instead of admiring the most serious and learned, are content with irresponsible teachers who hand everyone a pass … !

Was this how I came to be on good terms with my older sister? We drink together. At first we run down our gadabout mother. Then comes the moment when whatever she says is quite incomprehensible. When I start on my usual sermon, 'The superficial Turk, Turkey becoming shallow …', she passes out. And I pass out too as I whisper Kierkegaard and Wittgenstein in her ear …

Yesterday morning a bright light leapt from the mirror and, spiralling to a point, settled in my brain. The pleasant ache in my head turns into a spiritual and physical drugged condition which I will certainly make my friend …

Forty years on I've managed nevertheless not to 'suffer in silence'. With my mother and my students and the contemptible faculty of deans, I fight viciously and continuously. I'm certainly on the point of making peace with my loneliness. Am I releasing my pain before the dilemma increases? First I resisted the build-up of chaos, then I discovered why I couldn't escape from it. I'm dragged into depression, into the eye of the storm which Nietzsche and other philosophers reached. Masochistically I anticipate the arrival of the process and the last act. Waiting for my recovery, I take refuge in the aphorisms of Elias Canetti.

ભ

It was another Saturday when the holiday spirit was missing. Rezzan and I set off together in the direction of centrally located Şişli. I was curious about the son who was said to be 'depressed'. I entered the monastery-like La Paix Hospital praying, I don't know why. A nurse looking like a chronically ill patient showed us into a private visiting room and warned us in advance, 'You can stay for an hour, but don't excite the Hodja, Rezzan.'

I was just settling into the flimsy chair when the door creaked open and Gürsel Ergene entered, in his pale tracksuit inscribed with a 'Berkeley' logo in big letters. With a shudder I noticed that he resembled my first victim. Like a tiger just released from its cage, he looked shiftily round the room; he watched me and grinned while Rezzan paid him a string of stale compliments. He approached, dragging his slippers as he was informed that I was the well-heeled tenant who worked on a magazine and also dealt in secondhand books. Obstinately refusing to notice his mother, he watched me suspiciously, like a spoiled child who sees a panda for the first time. (I was beginning to regret the visit.) Then he said distinctly in a high-pitched voice, 'You read my diary, so you thought you'd like to see what this nutty man was like, my tormented friend.'

'Not at all, sir! ...' I began to sweat.

'Although you're got up like Lennie in *Of Mice and Men*, you have the look of an executioner,' he said, and continued to peer into my face as though he was examining coffee grounds to tell a fortune.

Did I hang my head? I felt as if a soothsayer had counted the names of all my victims in turn.

'The executioner is as much of a misunderstood volunteer as the philosopher or the poet,' he said, solemnly as a judge explaining his decision to acquit.

He sat before me, rocking to and fro. He was clearly pleased, behaving as though his mother wasn't there. He could read your humble servant like a wily psychologist. When he heard my view that the bigots and pseudo-intellectuals were insulting our religion, and heard moreover my attitude to wearing a turban and to revealing garments, he said, 'You are a pure neo-Islamist,' and I was almost as pleased as on the day I got promoted to sergeant.

He bent conspiratorially towards my left ear and asked, 'Would you like to hear an answer to any question in your mind now?', and I fell into his trap.

'I've always been curious, sir, about how many different languages are spoken on our planet.'

'Almost 6,000. After 100 years – 3,000 if the oil wells don't dry up first – eventually perhaps we'll whisper 500 languages. Now I have a two-part question, my tormented friend: would you rather catch your wife in bed with your cousin or catch her with your cousin's wife?'

I was beginning to pray 'God give me strength!' and Gürsel Hodja to tremble and giggle. His mother summoned the duty nurse, who took his arm and led him away respectfully, asking, 'Dear Hodja – shall I ask you a riddle you can't unravel, or a puzzle you can't answer?'

ଔ

'I've a bit of a headache,' Rezzan excused herself the following Saturday, and sneaked off to play bridge, so I took her son clean underwear and a spare tracksuit.

Gürsel Hodja sensed this might be the start of a long friendship and asked, 'I wonder if you're going to make me better or am I going to drive you mad?'

I poured out my heart to him, telling him about everything except my victims and my connection with Mecruh. I hoped it would boost his morale. He made no comment, and I listened to sad anecdotes he had omitted from his diary. This time it broke my heart to hear how his mother, then his whole world, had wasted the life of this fragile, talented personality. I was ashamed of my own bitter complaints in the face of his. I was ashamed of the shallow system that had failed to recognize his originality.

When I left I kissed his hand respectfully. He was surprised and blushed bright red like an orator embarrassed by applause. He thrust a piece of paper into my pocket, asking me to bring him a list of books from his library next time and, as a footnote, a croissant from the Konak Cake Shop.

He began to address me as 'Tiger' and his mother reduced her formal visits to once a month. I noticed he was in two minds about whether he should welcome or regret our growing friendship. Rezzan was found dead in her bed on the morning of 10 November, on the same day, sixty-seven years ago, that her secret enemy, Atatürk, passed away, and I was startled to note she was being buried in a plot opposite the gravestone of my first guilt-ridden victim. It fell to me to let my Hodja know he had lost his mother. What a disturbing duty that was, by God. He tried not to laugh.

Before the forty days of mourning that followed Rezzan's death were up, her daughter Emel made peace with her feeble husband Lemi. They and their Down's syndrome son, whose existence I'd not heard of before, settled in my basement. Renan, the eternal idler, began to drop by to see his nephew. Emel had undoubtedly given up drinking. She didn't scold Lemi as often as I expected and went to work every day, but only at noon. The boorish Lemi had retired as a public library official (I'd never seen him holding a book) and seemed to be devoting his time to their silent son. The whimsical youngster, who did not look his seventeen years, compared me to tough guy Sylvester Stallone, for heaven's sake! While his steely eyes, so like his uncle's, were closed in his strange noonday nap, his father could go out on the balcony with his rakı and lute. I enjoyed listening to him humming those songs with their plaintive melodies. An early part of his repertoire, which I had never heard before, was a sad unfamiliar song, which began, 'My lute became a stringed instrument, my heart became inflamed.' After a sip of rakı he would sigh deeply and whisper obscenities to the sea. And I was glad he was a man with no moustache.

ᗒ

News came of the death of the landlord of a landmark building on Eşrefsaat Street.

While the widow of the deceased married his young partner and before they had put up the sign 'For Rent', I moved in. I furnished my new place with Gürsel Hodja's books.

A couple of Canadian teachers, retired from some lycée or other, rented my old apartment. I told Emel that I would meet the expenses of the Hodja's care, and that the rent from the flat could go towards her son's schooling.

She embraced me joyfully and asked me to take all her brother's books from the library to my new home. I knew that Gürsel wouldn't be impressed when moved into the hospital's most luxurious room.

I had moved his books into boxes with fastidious care. Next to an autobiographical *Harem Life* was the diary of poor Sim Yetkin, the previous tenant, a lady no one remembered because she had committed suicide.

An assistant editor responsible for features in a weekly magazine, she had taken her own life at thirty. Again and again I read through the personal and courageous notes of this strange writer, who fell into a depression because she could not write poetry to her heart's content. I had read and been moved by the collected works of the popular – and suicidal – female poets. I refrained from telling my Hodja how impressed I was by lines that duelled with death at every turn. I chose extracts from the diary's beginning as, word by word, it circled nearer to her death, and I entered it for a short story competition in a monthly literary review, under the pseudonym, Sima Etkin, with the title, 'I Want to Write When I Read / I Read When I Cannot Write.' I knew we would win. Exploring the area round the Maiden's Tower, I may have heard behind me her shrill scream mingled with prayers, swallowed up by the sea. I wasn't surprised to hear from Bereket Market's shop assistant that 'the fat lady with spectacles who read a book even while she was buying cheese' had thrown herself into the sea in front of the Maiden's Tower.

❧

After his mother's death, Gürsel Hodja was freed of any guilt except for his thought-crime. I counted the days till Saturday, when I could stay with him for three hours if I wished. I did his washing with pleasure, and while choosing a sweatshirt for him I'd live through the stress of imagining Rezzan's criticism.

Released from his shackles, he was like a learned orator and a living encyclopedia of the social sciences. I listened with patience and respect, and my self-confidence increased every time we parted as though I had won a further diploma. He was as healthy psychologically as yours truly. I gradually decided he was less restless than any other city-dweller, including his doctor, and believed that Gürsel Ergene, the master philosopher, had seen the whole city turn into an insane asylum and had taken refuge in an obscure hospital for the good of his soul.

A

I no longer felt like searching for Dalga street by street. Through Selçuk Altun I managed to obtain the phone numbers of two of her confidantes, İdil and Serap. I felt uncomfortable at the chilly response of these one-time volleyball players, whom I remember screaming and leaping up to smash the ball. They told me about Dalga, how she left for England, then came back and stopped seeing her friends. Her mother married and moved to Toulouse and probably her grandfather was dead.

Disappointed at my failure, but pleased I had tried, I withdrew to the house. I was reading through all the poetry books in the library and at the same time translating Eugenio Montale in the evenings. (According to my father, poetry was the highest form of literature. The pleasure of interpreting had to be experienced, for every line had its sense of balance and form.) I went to bed with the morning ezan and even with the aid of a sleeping pill found it hard to sleep. Just as my eyes were closing I would be startled by the synchronized drips from all the taps in the house. Then a pair of feet would descend from on high and, with heavy steps, survey the rooms inch by inch, eventually slipping into my bedroom. Was it my mother's ghost? If I happened to be reading Küçük İskender I'd hide the book in the commode drawer before she started to fume with anger …

My Atatürk-loving grandfather was found dead in his bed on the morning of 11 November. As the founder of the Turkish Republic had passed away on 10 November, my naive uncle Salvador had whispered in my ear, 'I wish he had died the day before.'

ભ

The first primrose setting fire to the New Year set my head spinning, and I couldn't remember why I had come to distant Levent Market. I called the eternally lazy driver Hayrullah, and went home. Once I had taken my sedative pill, İfakat handed me an envelope. The sender of the blue envelope from London was Dalga Bayley.

Dear Arda,

I hear you've been looking for me – that gives me courage.

I must see you. I'm not ready to come back to Istanbul. (And I may never come back!)

If you're prepared to hear the worst possible scenario and you think you'll be able to look me in the face afterwards, then please come …

D

I was expecting freedom after my mother's death but I seemed to have become the prisoner of a sinister void. 'Is there any news that can possibly increase this boredom of mine?' I wondered, as I jotted down Dalga's address and phone number. I was expecting this disastrous and incomprehensible news to be an antidote to my struggle in the void.

At the airport I hid when I saw one of my mother's arrogant friends. I had had enough of reproaches for being still unmarried. The London flight was full of the English going home for Christmas. To avoid unnecessary conversations, I took refuge in *Goldberg Pasha*, by the writer Erje Ayden, who had remained in New York for the past forty-seven years without a passport. As the plane took off, I glanced at the beloved old city of Istanbul from high above. Apart from the Bosphorus and the Golden Horn, what I saw didn't even have the charm of a bedouin village. I was startled to recall that, according to research done by the municipality, sixty-nine per cent of the population lived below the breadline. I preferred to concentrate on the superficial stewardesses pacing back and forth, as if the plane would plummet to earth without them.

I met Dalga in the lobby of the family hotel Le Meridien in Piccadilly. She looked more haggard than I expected but was still smart and attractive. It was strange to see she still walked like a tomboy, ready to leap up and smash a volleyball if it appeared on the horizon. Considering what she had written in her note, I was prepared for a semi-formal embrace, though I would have loved to feel the scent of her body once again.

She suggested going up to my room. She threw her suede coat on the bed and took a bottle of whisky from the minibar. We sat opposite each other, wondering, suspicious. She made me talk but I doubt if she took anything in. I was beginning to feel ill-at-ease seeing her own increasing embarrassment. On her fourth attempt to light the cigarette she'd taken from her crumpled packet of Dunhill, she started on her tirade:

'I'm going to get straight to the point and you mustn't ask any questions. I have a knife in my bag in case you get disgusted and assault me.

'Arda, from the time I was fifteen until he died, I was your father's lover. He had this Sean Connery look that made every woman's heart beat faster. His voice was particularly attractive. My mother, even my distressed auntie, admired him. Like a part-time Lolita I managed to seduce him by entering his room under the pretext of studying. In his room we'd be content with foreplay but we had passionate get-togethers in the houses of his bachelor friends. He was happy with my admiration and I was happy when he made me feel important by sharing his troubles. Every time we met I felt I'd grown up a year.

'He complained that your mother's character changed after your birth. "In front of other people she showed me the respect due to a scholar or a sheikh, but she exhausted me with her problems and with making love. If she saw me fearful and ready to break because of her malice, she'd suddenly turn into an angel to stop me from running away," he said. "None of my scientific achievements made me as happy as becoming a father. If I took my baby son in my arms, she'd become as malevolent as a reptile. As Arda grew, her jealousy increased, and she began to abuse the poor boy whenever I got close to him. Sadly I became used to the idea of loving my son at a distance, hoping that distance would protect him, yet I couldn't totally withdraw." He thought you were smarter than him and that due to your dysfunctional family, you'd chosen to conceal your genius by maturing fast to escape an oppressive childhood. I think we both knew that sooner or later your mother would catch us. She learned about our relationship the summer of my last year at high school. Now all she had to do was provoke my enraged grandfather. When he heard of the latest disaster, my grandfather gave us a lump sum of money and kicked us out. "I don't want to see your faces ever again, you low-life whores," he said. We took refuge with my mother's cousin, who lived alone in her tiny flat in the quiet district of Erenköy. While I put up with this hotbed of developments, I thought it strange that my mother was cross with me, as she herself was the mistress of a young married colleague.

'Almost immediately after she broke free from her house arrest my mother started to blossom. She met an old flirt at a New Year's party for her faculty friends and her fate took a turn for the better. They married quickly. Her new husband lived in Paris. After his aging first wife had died, he'd inherited a gourmet restaurant and a wine company. The day I got my half-term report, my mother left for Toulouse, I received an acceptance from the Psychology Department at King's College, and my stepfather offered to support me financially.

'The following week your father phoned to wish me a happy birthday and I thought my heart would stop. I was always in his mind, he told me, but he hadn't called, imagining I'd be busy preparing for the university entrance exam. Once it was certain that I'd be leaving for London to become a student, we began to meet again. I was waiting for him in a desolate house in the next street when he was shot down before a mosque wall. I left for London five days later, and after the first shock I tried to reflect on what had happened. From what your mother said to the police, which was reflected in the press, it seems your father was being threatened by some fundamentalists. But that was a complete sham. I'd never heard a single word from Mürsel about any such threat, and he never hid anything from me. What about the name of this group who supposedly assassinated him? They had never been involved in any operation before. As for your father, who thought there was no problem in the world he couldn't solve, except women, he had slipped up somewhere or other and aroused your mother's suspicions. He kept on saying, "If this woman doesn't kill me with her baleful looks, she'll have it done by someone else." The last couple of times we met he had the feeling we were being followed.

'You can't deny that your mother was cruel and vindictive. I think that when Mürsel had his last chance and blew it, she had him killed.

'I can see you're shaken, but I thought I'd no right to hide what I knew from you.'

Happy to be relieved of the load she'd been carrying so long, she grabbed another bottle from the minibar and making two attempts to light her cigarette, tried to gauge my reaction. I'd been shocked to hear of my father's forbidden passion for my childhood love, but I was even more appalled at the possibility that my mother had had my father murdered. (Was I going to be buried under another wave of depression?) Then Dalga started on her farewell speech: 'It took me two years to recover from a series of depressions; they all began with my guilty conscience. I went into intensive therapy and graduated from school a year late. Professor Tom Bayley, vice-dean of the department, had supported me during the crisis, and when Tom and his American wife eventually divorced, we married as soon as I graduated. My husband is 18 years older than I am, and reminds me a little of your dad; I have a son named Adrian who is now five years old. (I couldn't find an English name closer to Arda.) How fond I was of you, Arda. In my dreams I would fly with you and Mürsel and descend on an island where we lived happily ever after. I knew you had mixed feelings about me. I knew you were peeping when I was taking a shower after sunbathing, and to tantalize you even more I'd especially pose for you.

'I wanted to see you after your mother's death but I never felt strong enough. Only Serap knew my address and what had happened to me. I had warned her not to give away my secret, so she got rid of you. Then I began to believe in fate, perhaps to console myself after all that had happened. If you hadn't called I'm sure we would never have met like this, or might have met at a less significant time.

'By pouring out my heart I've darkened yours. How about joining us at eight o'clock tomorrow night for Christmas dinner, so we can share some cheerful stories for a change? You can meet my husband, my stepdaughter Ethel and my son who thinks you're his uncle. I'd understand if you decided we shouldn't meet again, but you must know that I cherish your friendship, Arda …'

I sat motionless when Dalga left the room. Eyes closed, I was wondering what my father's killer was doing at that very moment. Instead of finishing off the row of drinks in the minibar, I (like mother, like son) swallowed a Valium and a half and escaped to bed.

CR

I knew I would wake up depressed after a sleep that lasted only three hours. Suppose Dalga had asked, 'Why did you try to call me after so many years?' While thinking of an answer I realized I had an erection. (When my mother used to say, 'Salvador sent these,' as she handled the pornographic magazines in their plastic bags, I would notice how self-sacrificing she sounded. Whenever we came to London we stayed at this hotel in Piccadilly, which is almost next door to sleazy Soho. A tip from the reception-desk, and she would shoo me off to the nearest strip club, to be back in two hours.)

Instead of dining I finished off the crackers in the minibar. I dropped by Waterstone's bookshop opposite the hotel and stayed in the gay and poetry sections until it closed. Somehow my feet led me to Soho just as quickly and nervously as they had done seven years before and I found the 'Down Down Club' as easily as if I had been there only seven days before. The corridor stank of urine. In a room reeking of vomit there were some twenty men – young Arabs and Japanese and older Englishmen. I was afraid to sit in the very front row next to the cylindrical stage, where five sulky-looking beauties were taking turns to dance. The young men rose from their seats and slid

£5 notes into the girls' garters and snatched kisses as a reward.

During the break some courageous punters bought drinks for the most popular girls, Tiffany, Paloma, Amanda, Venus and Pandora. Long-legged Tiffany, with her pierced blonde pubes, reminded me of the movie goddess Nicole Kidman. While she stripped to tunes sung by Tina Turner and Chris Rea, the £20 note I was holding was soaked with sweat. I got up to leave, cursing myself for not having the courage to advance a few steps and touch her. I knew I would be treated as a pervert by the bouncer when I left the sleazy dive early.

I dozed off reading *Any Human Heart*, William Boyd's novel of a life, in diary form. Near morning I woke with a start to hear drunken howls from the street. And I set out to contemplate the chilling problem of how one human being could be capable of spraying another with bullets.

જી

I was startled to realize how eager I was to meet the Bayley family. The nearer I got to the address in Sloane Avenue, with its rows of brick buildings, the more apprehensive I became. At the door of the big two-storey edifice, in front of which a Rover was parked, I nervously examined the select champagne and the silver frame I was carrying. I quickly removed my finger from the buzzer when I heard from within a loving dialogue between Dalga and her half-English, half-Turkish son. I shut my eyes tight as the ache in my forehead began to throb with Adrian's giggles. Maybe afraid of falling in love with Dalga again, or of identifying with her husband, I left the packages at the door and began to run down the street.

As I reached King's Road I noticed a plaque on the wall: 'George Seferis (1901–1971), Nobel Prize winner, Greek poet and Ambassador, lived here.' I felt as happy as if I had bumped into a fellow countryman, but embarrassed when I recalled the chauvinist politician from Urla, the poet's home town in Turkey, who had tried to rename Seferis Street. My father, may he rest in peace, had always said, 'If Oktay Rifat had been a Greek poet he would have won the Nobel Prize a long time ago.'

God bless human beings who remain indoors for the sake of Christmas! I enjoyed walking through the deserted streets till I reached Sloane Square tube station. There were only two of us waiting for the train. In a situation like this I usually acknowledge the other person, and encouraged by his sad face I asked the young chap with the antique accordion, 'Are you Romanian?' He replied, 'Are you Russian?' After we had both identified ourselves I gave Pavel from Prague a £20 note and said, 'Play me your favourite piece.'

Hesitantly he announced Dvořák's 'Songs My Mother Taught Me', and began to sing in a high voice. When I realized the depth of love and yearning in those melancholy lines, of which I understood not a word, my heart grew sad. For the first time listening to a song, I felt I must close my eyes. Maybe because I didn't know how to laugh, I knew I wasn't going to cry. The damned train arrived before the song ended and Pavel and I got into the same carriage. I gave him another twenty and asked him to keep on playing the same piece till we reached Piccadilly Circus. Through this old melody which lasts only three minutes, I realized what had been missing from my whole life.

With a lighter heart, I got off at Piccadilly Circus. I wasn't surprised when I lost my footing and slipped and fell at the bottom of endless stairs. As I fell to the ground I was embarrassed to hear screams. I landed on my left palm and knee and closed my eyes to avoid seeing the crowd around me but when I heard a friendly woman asking, 'Are you all right?', my pain seemed to increase. Dragging my left foot and blowing on my hand, I reached a bench at the end of the platform, sat down and began to cry. I threw my sodden tissue towards the noisy mice on the tracks before heading for the main exit. I thought I was able to walk better in spite of the pain in my knee, and just as my uncle would have advised, I kept my shoulders back, my head up, and looked fifty metres ahead. I was almost free of the hazy veil over my eyes. When my grey blurred surroundings began to appear in their true colours, it seemed as if my chemistry had changed. I headed for my room with hope. The more I walked the better I felt. I multiplied two six-figure numbers in my head and checked the result with a calculator. (Unfortunately I wasn't wrong.) I took refuge in *Any Human Heart*, but lost interest when the narrator met the Prince of Wales, who abdicated for love of the woman he eventually married. Wasn't my father's book that I had found amongst 'Songs My Mother Taught Me' an autobiography of the confused king? I felt uneasy as I realized the meaningless connection and rushed out. You probably thought I would go to the Down Down and plant a £5 note on Tiffany. But turning into a deserted New Bond Street, where I used to die of boredom walking with my mother, I was about to take a momentous decision: I was going to find my father's killer!

B

'Allah loves those who have been cleansed.'
Tevbe:108

'The man who was so good he forgot his own name.'
'Don't tell me who you are. I want to worship you.'
'We are hypocrites because we cannot forget the things we have acquired.'
'Is it not sadder to be renewed than to disappear?'
'Words used once a lifetime. Which ones?'
'Eternity as a comet …'
'All that is written is out of date before the ink is dry.'

On my three-hundredth visit to Gürsel Hodja he greeted me with, 'Choose seven aphorisms of Elias Canetti, translate them into Turkish, write your own paraphrase of each, and bring them to our next meeting.' (Yours truly struggled hard with the lines above.) He wanted me, God bless him, to invent comic and epic stories from his depressing sketches. (That was how your humble servant realized that writing is harder than pulling the trigger.)

I noticed he was trying to give me guidance without undermining my knowledge. My Hodja wanted to think that every meeting had some influence on me, otherwise I wouldn't come. While time was erasing my impetuous tendencies, my secret cells were coming to life. If I glimpsed an erotic poster from the corner of my eye I would dream I was descending into the vaults of the unclean. One evening, tired of reading, I found myself unable to turn away at the last minute from the front door of a brothel, God be praised!

Is it because I can't swim that I respect the sea? If there was no threat of rain or whiff of snow, I walked to the wharf and on the crossing between Üsküdar and Beşiktaş my eagerness to meet my Hodja grew stronger. Ottoman postcards of the old ferry-boats still conveyed the grave forgotten dignity of our forefathers, and journeys of fifteen minutes began and ended with the splendour of a transatlantic crossing. On my last visit to Gürsel Hodja, while I was concentrating on a newspaper article by Taha Kıvanç, I was distracted by a large book left on the bench to my right. The title of the work was *The People's King*, and it examined King Edward VIII's wish to abdicate for love of the American widow he wanted to marry.

'Since he was king and wanted to marry a widow, why didn't he trust to the people's support?' – this was the question I wanted to put to the Hodja.

According to the name-plate, the book on the ferry belonged to Selçuk Altun, whose novels Taha Kıvanç had recommended. The man whose works I swore I'd never read was said to be on the board of directors of a private bank.

◌

Head louse Baybora's latest announcement was as follows: 'Chief gunslinger, we'll meet in the Park of the Turkish Women's Union at two o'clock tomorrow to bring about justice and take $100,000 and her prayers from a tearful but wealthy lady.'

After this final episode your humble servant swore that he would bump off this creep Baybora. (I ground my teeth every time I heard his voice.) As there is no word for 'resign' in our line of business, to break free I had to reach the boss glorified by the title 'Executioner'– if he actually existed. Undoubtedly I was being taken for a ride! I never came across crimes like mine in the news. Instead of a gang, there were perhaps two crooks who took yours truly for a fool. Besides, I had lost my enthusiasm for the job, though not my discipline. After every episode the Hodja would greet me with, 'You're looking shifty again, like someone who has just cheated on his mate.'

Baybora chose the lonely hours of shady local parks to meet and confer. In the stunted little park of peaceful Acıbadem there was a sculpture of two young children and their sad, lovelorn mother. I was tracing the signature of the work when the louse suddenly appeared with a sneer: 'I'm not surprised you're looking at a statue with hidden thighs and breasts.' He handed me a dossier as though he was awarding me a prize but I had no wish to examine it.

ભ

On this occasion I did not submit to the dossier's information with a respectful prayer. As soon as I saw the photograph of my next victim Soner İlkin, I grew nervous. The doomed wretch, who seemed to be in his forties, had an arrogant bearing, as though he'd been his own sculptor. This would be the last time, please God, that my left hand looked for trouble.

I was expecting the parasite to be married to a wealthy businesswoman older than himself, but I was not expecting him to have seduced his wife's two daughters, one by her first husband, and married, the other by her second husband, and a schoolgirl. The pervert was on the board of his wife's export firm. Despite warnings, he couldn't resist withdrawing massive advances from the company funds, losing money on the stock exchange and gambling. He used his trade secrets for blackmail, and for his divorce he demanded half the company's main assets. His wife's detective reported that her dissolute husband was with a couple of Ukrainian prostitutes on a yacht anchored at Göcek Bay in the Mediterranean.

I was sure that 'trade secrets' included falsification of documents, unregistered documents, tax evasion. (Once again I was thankful that I had nothing to do with the stinking business world.)

I flew to Dalaman and booked into the Seren Guesthouse, its entrance hall resonant with sad laments. Next morning my package was delivered to me, stamped 'special tourist material'. Hidden between a prayer rug and decorative saddlebags were the dismantled parts of a telescopic rifle (SV99) and as I prayed and reassembled the piece, I was as happy as if I'd met one of my army friends.

I made lonely Göcek, twenty minutes away by minibus, my base. On the eve of the town's tourist season it had retreated into a spring siesta. I was amazed that the miniature main road wasn't filled with commotion. The gigantic yacht *Sürtük* was moored between Göcek Island and the strip of shore that belonged to the Forestry Commission. I kept watch for seventy-two hours, and from the grove of irregular pine trees that reached the summit my eye followed inch by inch the agent of sin. Every time my hand made a move towards the heavy field-glasses I saw the bow of the boat shaking. I won't go into details about the lecherous behaviour of sinister Soner and the voluptuous prostitutes in the gunwale (I felt some sympathy for the one without sunglasses, because she took every opportunity to read a book).

The shameless Soner was videoing the naked love scenes between the two helpless girls as I clutched the SV99 with the silencer.

My left eye covered the telescopic sight. The rifle, your humble servant and the ground had all merged into one. With a silent prayer I marked the target, and as my arms seemed to lengthen and reach inside the yacht, I emptied the magazine into the head and chest of the dishonourable wretch. The prostitutes threw themselves screaming into the sea and I ran zigzagging to the shore, where I dismantled the gun and, as the pieces sank into the dark sea, leapt into the copse. Running to the town square, I remembered that the son-in-law of a media mogul had been shot in the same place last year. (I wondered if my fellow assassin had disappeared in the same way.)

∞

I was sure that the swaggering Baybora would hand over his final payment with the words, 'Has it ever occured to you how many thousand girls you could pull in for sex with this money?' (Yours truly sent one third of his earnings to the Society for the Protection of Historic Works in Üsküdar.)

For the first time in my life I set off on a very long journey. I took in Master Ahmet Hamdi Tanpınar's favourite cities (Ankara, Bursa, Konya and Erzurum) and, tipped off by Ibn Battuta, I included historic Alanya. When I returned I felt as if I'd made a pilgrimage to Mecca before dying.

CR

At the conclusion of our meetings in the lonely parks, Baybora would expect me to leave first so it would be impossible for me to follow him. But for this last commission I brought along the driver, Hozatlı Veli, as my assistant. I had rescued him from three religious fanatics who attacked him for smoking during Ramadan. Cross-eyed Veli, lurking in the shade, followed Baybora to his headquarters in Üsküdar's Fıstıkağacı district, and from the meeting-places Baybora chose I guessed he lived on the Anatolian side. I decided to set up base in Müneccimbaşı Street, which had no Ottoman legacy and was luckily not frequented by wealthy people dressed up as dandies or thieves. While we have so many splendid streets with forgotten names, I was pained to see neighbouring streets named 'Yapma Bebek' (Baby Doll) or 'Su Deposu' (Water Depot).

I knew I would dislike Baybora's house. The façade looked as though it hadn't seen a coat of paint since it was built and in the claustrophobic courtyard a stunted cedar tree and an old car passed the time together in harmony. Once I learned his real name I didn't think I'd need to inspect his life closely. While Veli and his gaudy taxi were on the lookout on the hill next to Nimet Doughhouse, I was remembering how my mother had never managed to fry the meat pasties to the right consistency. I ordered Veli to get out of his car and called Baybora on my mobile.

'What's up, chief, were we partying in your dreams, or what?' he said.

'A guy called Tufan rang me on this phone and asked me to join a new gang they're setting up. They'll pay a transfer fee of $500,000 and thirty per cent higher wages. Perhaps you've had wind of this?'

'I hope you can hear yourself. So what did you say, Bedirhan?'

'I didn't have to say anything. He said he'd call in forty-eight hours to get my answer. He spoke as if your gang was breaking up anyway.'

'And where are you now, my brave friend?'

'At home.'

'Take care – don't move. We'll meet up in three hours at the latest.'

I knew he would immediately pass on my mischief-making message to the Executioner and that it would explode before him like a hand grenade. My aim was to make Baybora suspicious of his boss. We crossed to the European side, pursuing the grey Audi that Baybora mistreated like a poor old mule. Climbing the outskirts we reached the hills of Arnavutköy. He parked his vehicle on Beyazgül Street sloping down to the Bosphorus under a banner headed, 'Third Suspension Bridge: Hayır, No, Nein,

Non.' I laughed at his comical hopping walk and thought he might roll over. I sent Veli off and tailed Baybora.

I felt at home in the quiet street, as charming as market-places in the old Turkish films of the sixties, recalling a time long gone when life was relaxed and unhurried. Among the competing shop signs, the kebab shops clearly won the day. But as I approached the shore the Anatolian character of the market diminished, and it angered me to see a man from the Black Sea swaggering into the bakery.

Baybora turned right into the deserted Dubaracı Street, which was more beautiful than a dream. A narrow lane led uphill and was embellished with tall, well-kept timber houses, their balconies overhanging the street. I shivered in the name of my unresolved loneliness. The climb came to an end when I reached the turquoise-painted narrow façade of a tiny mansion. Baybora looked around, then leant on the doorbell. He entered, pushing aside the sturdy woman in an apron who opened the door. (I had four candidates in mind as Executioner.) Respectfully checking the Walther XIV hidden in my parka, I gave myself ten minutes to plan a raid on the mansion. Then the main door flew open, and a maid in her burgundy coat ran towards the side street. Did the Executioner prefer to meet his assistant alone? I approached and settled down to wait until the door opened and I could jump in. A little later, when I had raped the tired old lock with a pick, as Baybora would have put it, I found myself in a spacious living room. Baybora's angry voice penetrated a crack in the half-glazed door and as I approached I pricked up my ears.

'Faking or not, for the last five years I've been telling you to get rid of this half-wit. Just give me the word and I'll take out this melancholic faggot …' I could hardly wait till he finished his sentence. I plunged into the room and fired four bullets into the neck and ugly head of this vile fellow, whose real name I had never known in twelve years. I was astonished to see that the trembling man behind the antique table was Baki Kutay, my old master, the retired colonel and book restorer. He began to sob. I was embarrassed and sat down to wait in the seat Baybora had just vacated.

My finger was still on the trigger as Baki wiped away his tears with the sleeve of his stylish jumper and started to breathe through his nose.

'It's shame that made me cry, Bedirhan, not fear,' he said. 'Even if you're not curious to know how I ended up like this, I'll tell you anyway. Then you'll put an end to my pain with a single bullet, all right, son?

'Though they call me "Colonel" I was actually a major when I was thrown out of the army. My wife died of a brain haemorrhage while we were on manoeuvres at sea. They said she would have had a chance if I'd been with her, and when my handicapped daughter, who was very attached to her, fell into a deep depression I gradually began to lose my mind.

'I was discharged from the army on grounds of

unsuitability. No sooner was I free to enjoy rare books and Sufi music than I had news of the death of my naval officer son at sea. I'd always objected to his profession. Now I had to be strong and fight for the well-being of my grandchild. You yourself witnessed how I didn't give up even when my right arm was put out of action. But when I heard that Dalga, whom I'd nurtured so carefully when she was a young schoolgirl, had become the lover of a professor old enough to be her father, I gave up. I kicked her out with her flirt of a mother and took refuge in alcohol. The paedophile professor's wife was a close neighbour to me. Three months later she came to my house sobbing bitterly. She said that now Dalga had started an affair with her husband, we must find a way to at least save her son and my grandchild.

'She was seething with hate and when she said she was prepared to pay $1 million to free herself from Mürsel forever, I asked for forty-eight hours to think about it.

'People who are keen on books and materialistic never have any problem finding an excuse. Ada Ergenekon's proposal could be my first and last chance to combat the series of misfortunes that were destroying me. You and Emin, whom you know as Baybora, came to mind. I've always sensed a natural killer in your introverted personality, which may be genetic. Emin was my wife's cousin, may she rest in peace; when he was shot during an operation he couldn't accept minor police duties. He was unreliable and ambitious but while he waited to retire he had made crucial contacts in the underworld and the security forces. While investigating you we heard about the Tarlabaşı raid and our appetite was whetted. With the money I made from shooting the professor, I bought this mansion and Emin set out at once to furnish it properly. Hale committed suicide when she learned of the filthy business I'd got mixed up in, but still we wouldn't come to our senses. Thanks to your mother, I could achieve some of the things I'd been unable to for lack of money. For the last five years, Emin has been warning me to put an end to the business, but if I'd agreed I would have been signing your death warrant too. Believe me, I couldn't do that to you. Besides, I was curious to know where all this would lead.

'And you turned out to be smarter than we thought, Bedirhan. I've lived a life of ups and downs and I'm exhausted. Today is my seventy-seventh birthday – whatever bullets you've left me as a present, son, I'm ready for them ...'

'Listen, master,' I said, 'although I've realized for years that I was being manipulated by one or two smart people, I've never reacted. We staged a play in thirteen acts and I believe I've had the most fun. Last month when I reached my thirty-seventh birthday and failed to celebrate it, I vowed to get to you for the final act. In spite of our forty years' age difference I don't feel any less tired or less guilty than you. There are enough bullets for both of us in this gun I'm putting in front of you. I'm giving you the chance to rid this planet of one or two filthy parasites ...'

He lifted the gun with his left hand and for a while he talked to himself. Did he try to laugh? I knew when I turned round and headed for the door that my master would choose to celebrate his birthday with a single bullet.

It was as though there'd been a blackout on Dubaracı Street. I turned into Beyazgül Street where an old fishmonger was setting up his stand.

'You've taken care of the parasites, now it's time to settle your own account, Bedirhan,' I said to myself on my way down to the shore. I had the courage to realize that another whirlwind of excitement was heading my way. I was being swept up by the pleasure of fighting a duel with myself.

I was happy when I remembered my meeting with Gürsel Hodja next morning. My first task was to ask him if the word 'melancholic' was an insult or not. Suddenly I felt as if I hadn't slept for twelve years. I found a taxi, its windshield covered with giant beads against the evil eye. On the protective cloth cover of the driver's seat were the words, 'O Turkish youth! If you are a Fenerbahçe fan be proud; if not, submit.'

Your humble servant couldn't refrain from laughing, God forgive me!

A

My father used to be enraged by incompetent waiters who put on airs as if the customers might starve without them, by philistine librarians who couldn't read but did their best to discomfit booklovers, and by garrulous presenters of general-knowledge game shows, puffed up with pride as though they were the last surviving scholars on the planet. As for me, at the moment I can't stand those artificial-looking stewardesses who glide up and down the aisles like reluctant waiters.

The stewardess of the 'business class' section was presenting the flight security precautions with the usual repulsive mimicry. I watched the pantomime which she had perhaps repeated a thousand times, an object lesson in understanding 'how someone could be so persistently out of tune'. Although she was chewing gum, I warmed to the plump middle-aged lady in the seat next to me. She was coiled like a spring, ready to jump from her seat at any moment. She had the attractiveness that lies somewhere between beauty and ugliness; with her dark complexion and thick eyebrows, she seemed to be the daughter of a tribal chief from Eastern Turkey. I couldn't ask her if the elderly gentleman passed out on the seat to her right was her husband or not, but I gathered she was a princess descended from the thirty-fifth Ottoman Sultan, Mehmet Reşat. (Her great-great-grandfather's imperial watch is part of our family collection.)

I was anxious to tell my uncle what I had heard from Dalga. I'd missed the iodine-like smell of his claustrophobic attic flat in luxurious Maçka. I wasn't surprised to see Eric Gill's *25 Nudes* on the formica table in his pretentious living room. Uncle Salvador must have satisfied his weekly need for masturbation with the aid of these erotic drawings that were over sixty years old. I had to patiently listen to his observations on the Kangal Balıklı Spa before I could confide in him. He described how the eczema all over his body had been cleaned up in the thermal spring by a crazed school of fish, the largest 10 cm long.

He shook his head in disgust when he heard of the love between Dalga and my father, thankful he had remained a bachelor. Of the possibility that my mother had hired an assassin to kill my father, he said, 'It's not impossible. Maybe this was why Ada, instead of mourning after my brother-in-law's death, was devoured by feelings of guilt.

Arda, if your mother had gone to the doctor as soon as she noticed pain in her chest she wouldn't have died of cancer. She was inflicting a fatal punishment on herself by hiding her illness and didn't want you to guess that that was what she was doing.'

On the verge of a headache, I closed my eyes and held my sweating forehead. (Would anything I heard about my mother ever surprise me?) I had to start searching for my father's killer immediately. It didn't take long before I started to feel bad about concealing my aim from my uncle. Though I remembered that for the first time in my life I had reason to have feelings of self-respect, I was ashamed that my fate was driving me to an act of revenge.

When I rose to leave, my uncle, happy as a child on his way to the amusement park, started to tell me about his proposed trip to distant museums with El Greco paintings.

ଔ

On the pretext of bringing him the controversial books my mother had not been able to get rid of, I made my first – and last – visit to Selçuk Altun in his soulless office. I knew that when I asked for his help in getting detailed information about my father's police file he would give me the once-over and make me feel small. He made me an appointment for the next day with the director of a fashionable illustrated magazine of culture and the arts, which either flattered the party in power, if necessary, or blackmailed it if not. The lady, whose unusual name (İz Bozok) reminded me of Dalga's, would be able to help by introducing me to the legal correspondent of the conglomerate's newspaper. While he talked to her on the phone I examined a literary magazine named *Serendipity* from a pile of printed material on the next table. (And as I memorized the rules for entry to a poetry competition run by the magazine, a marvellous idea came into my head.)

In forty-five minutes starting from the evening ezan, I invented the following poem by choosing single lines in chronological order from each of Oktay Rifat's fifteen books of poems written between 1946 and 1987 – the title is my own:

Stolen

In the tumult of your life
In my nightly fantasies my daily thoughts
Never ask what is this blue
There's a salty sea-smell in the air
Like houses like rooms far off
Only doors remain poor doors
We hid in the deepest shadows,
At the window, I saw loneliness in the depths
A white cloth on the table, a copper bucket, then your face
Now no bright water, no green night
The moon was racing, cicadas chirp
Houses empty, empty light, empty streets

Not rough, not hurtful
The sea suddenly comes close
When I shut my eyes.

I read 'Stolen' twice and decided to try my hand at a free version of haiku also. From the titles of poems in the poet's last three books, namely *Speaking to the Sun*, *Naked and Dumb* and *A Great Summer*, I assembled the following in ten minutes:

Three Triplets

I
Candles and night
A tooth by the bedside
I leave to sleep

II
Poem's arrival told
Old letters
In the old armchair

III
Garden and sea
Marsh and sky
Leaves again.

(I sent in my collages to *Serendipity*'s competition. I thought the name Rifat Toktay and the attractive address I picked from the telephone directory – Eşrefsaat Street, Üsküdar – would bring me luck. When the results were published five weeks later I was not surprised to see that I had come first in both poetry competitions. The prize-winning short story I read was a poetic piece titled 'I Want to Write when I Read, I Read when I Cannot Write'. I was certain that Sima Etkin, the signature at the end of the story, was the pen name of the woman who had committed suicide because she couldn't live with what she had written. I was shocked when I saw that the address given was the now abandoned apartment block where Dalga's family had lived. Perhaps fate was telling me that I would find a writer instead of a hired killer.)

ை

The surly caretaker in Şehbender Plaza's noisy neighbourhood gave me a knowing look and directed me to the seventh floor. Beyond the swing door was a platform the size of an Olympic swimming pool with dozens of young people, mostly girls, running around in a panic. The widest area partitioned off by glass belonged to İz Bozok. I hesitated when I saw her leaning on the oval table and talking on the phone. My quick, searching gaze took in the long dark face and huge eyes of a short-haired young woman with a prominent forehead. I realized she had seen me and was waving me in with the ruler in her hand. As she rose without cutting off her conversation on the phone,

I thought her blue velvet trousers and blood-red shirt suited her tiny body. She gave me a soldier's salute as she laid down her ruler, then shook hands and pointed to the armchair nearest the desk, her lips miming 'Excuse me.' The sexy tone of her voice revealed a witty, incisive style, and I thought this was the kind of girl my father would have wanted for me. Noticing she had begun to examine me, I focused on the panel behind her on which hung a poster of a Sumo wrestler. I tried hard not to listen to the end of her conversation by distracting myself with the slogans on the poster above her desk: 'Citizen, Don't Ignore Those Who Spit on the Ground – Those Who Overlook the Law – Those Who Spoil Our Peace and Quiet – Those Who Show Every Kind of Disrespect. *The Society for War on Disrespect.*'

(My eyes congratulated the Bozok girl as she scolded the so-called painter who, not content with pulling strings to get an exhibition in a public gallery, was pressing her to arrange an interview in one of her magazines.) Noticing I wasn't smoking, she asked, 'Would you like a cup of rosehip tea as a reward?' I was ready for her question, 'Do you mind if I ask why you've waited twelve years to delve into the file on your father's assassination?'

'If I can, I want to write, or ask someone else to write, my father's biography. While my mother was alive I wasn't brave enough to take a long look at the detective part of the affair. I lost her recently and wanted to talk with the police before my enthusiasm for the project faded.'

'I'm very sorry about your father; it seems he was an incredible human being. He was not only a great scholar, but during the last fifteen years of his life it was his pronouncements on our progress and socio-economic conditions that reflected the state of our country best. I've heard that some of the television programmes he appeared in are now being used as material by university faculties of communication. He was certainly an oracle ...'

After immediate contradictory feelings of pride and humiliation, I was convinced that if fate had so decreed, this gamine of a girl would have been smitten with my father at first sight. We exchanged summaries of our lives until our insipid drinks were finished. (She was impressed by the fact that I hadn't become fodder for the paparazzi.)

She thrust a piece of paper into my hand as if she were giving me a tip, and I took that to mean that our first meeting was about to end. The piece of yellow paper the size of a visiting card carried the address of a shooting range in Altunizade; it belonged to the retired chief commissioner of police, Adil Kasnak ... I felt uneasy when I heard that he would expect me in his office after Friday prayers to discuss the Mürsel Ergenekon conspiracy.

İz Bozok accompanied me to the main door. Standing by the magazine name-plates, she said deprecatingly, 'Unfortunately we don't publish any magazine worthy of your calibre.' 'What other publications are there, apart from the satirical magazines?' I asked. On leaving her office I had noticed she was wearing ridiculous sandals with the Fenerbahçe logo. (My mother would have been horrified.) And it was then I decided to win over, any way I could, this delightful girl with whom I felt I had been friends for ten years.

'After you've seen the chief commissioner we can meet again. Don't hesitate to call.'

(In reality I wanted to say, 'Can I invite you home to discuss the results of the official meeting with the police and show you my father's library?') But as I foolishly watched her delicately scratching her knee, I heard myself murmuring, 'Thanks for your interest.'

ભ

I was taken aback when I saw the instructions, ('Get ready! Take aim! Fire!') as though I had arrived at the Abu Ghraib prison. But the ramshackle shooting range was as harmless-looking as a deserted police station. Suspiciously I approached the room from which the sound of music was floating through a half-open door. Behind a rough table under a wall sat Adil Kasnak, a massive hunk of a man, reminiscent of Anthony Quinn. His body spilled over the chair and seemed to be resting on the table as his left hand waved his amber prayer beads and summoned me in to him. Garish postcards were scattered on a glass coffee table next to the chair where I perched. Behind Kasnak was a portrait of a smiling Atatürk in a fur coat. (I felt myself begin to sweat.) In heavily accented Turkish he quizzed me about my life. As his eyes checked me over and he began to grin, I gave up explaining why I wanted to investigate my father's file. His bead-counting slowed down, he sighed noisily and, his body relaxed, he began to utter each separate word distinctly, as so many officials do.

'At the time of Professor Mürsel's murder I was a newly recruited superintendent in the Criminal Investigation Office. I followed the progress of his file until I retired and I even remember its number. The conspiracy had been planned by experts; they picked a suitable time for the event and a place that was isolated but near a main road, and not a single clue was left for the ballistic team to follow up. Your father, who was caught in front of the Rumi Mehmet Paşa Mosque, was often seen hurrying through the streets by people in the neighbourhood. We found your late father's jaunts through the dark byways of Üsküdar quite bizarre. Your mother fiercely denied the possibility of *une affaire de coeur* and claimed that he researched even stranger localities for his studies. God forgive me, but what an aggressive woman she was, she insisted emphatically that her husband had been threatened and shot by a gang of fanatics. According to her, your father had never taken the situation seriously enough to inform the police ...

'The so-called gang that undertook the job, and whose name I've forgotten, was never heard of again. But my gut instinct is that the event was not the work of a gang.

'I wonder if the soul of your father haunts you in your dreams because his death remains like a pair of his own unsolved equations, but I'm certain of one thing, that you personally want to find his killer.

'If you accidentally came across his killer I'm equally sure you wouldn't know what to do. Don't take offence, but even as you sit there listening to me, you look uneasy. You don't look like a young man of this country! You seem like someone who grew up in a time capsule till he was twenty. I'll bet you've used the exemption policy and paid up to postpone your military service for as long as it takes, and you've never handled even a toy gun. Did you ever get mixed up in street fights when you were a kid, or kick your opponent in a game of football, eh, you celebrated Ergenekon?

'Believe me, son, there's not a single clue in your father's dossier you can follow up. It's just a hypothesis of mine, but take a piece of advice from a Black Sea chap. The bigger the city of Istanbul grew, the more of a shallow village it became. That's why it's always the same three hundred people who attend official ceremonies, important concerts and exhibitions, the favourite restaurants and places of entertainment. I wonder if the city's underworld is any deeper and more sinister than we think. If five people were to find out you were looking for your father's killer, they'd be so keen to let others know, that the number would double in five minutes. You can be sure the second will exaggerate the story and pass it on immediately to twenty more. If the murderer or his organization are still in business, they'll hear the news faster than any news agency could broadcast it. If you think of the gossip doing the rounds of the banking and media worlds, the likelihood of my hypothesis increases. One evening when you go back to your mansion in a good mood, perhaps some bastard with a Kalashnikov will be waiting for you, son.

'I *strongly* recommend that you make friends with a gun. An academic makes a poor fighter but a good marksman. If you've picked up the slightest scientific knowledge from your father, within four months in our shooting range you might even be able to reach the level of one of our high-calibre marksmen. Then you'll find you've gained in self-confidence and learned eventually how to shoot without thinking, like a Zen philosopher. Finally, my son, guns are less dangerous to have as friends than women.

'We charge $240 a month for three sessions a week. If you don't ask for a receipt you'll get a 10 per cent discount and won't have to pay VAT.'

I took his visiting card with its crumpled corners, wondering if he'd used it to pick his teeth, and muttered that I would call him at the earliest opportunity. In front of Altunizade Mosque I took a taxi home, where I consulted a map of the city. It includes 48,000 streets and thoroughfares, and it didn't surprise me to find that Eşrefsaat, the address for the competition I had happened to choose from the telephone directory, was the street next to the mosque where my father was shot. Was this disaster or salvation approaching like a slow pestilence? I was shaken but not at all afraid. For therapy, I read W. H. Auden and T. S. Eliot.

◌

I felt almost guilty when I woke up without depression. Remembering it was already Thursday morning, I cut my nails. According to İfakat, cutting your nails on Monday meant you'd suffer torments, on Tuesday that your child would die, on Wednesday that bad news was in the offing, and to cut nails at night shortens life. I don't believe in superstitions, touch wood, but suppose İfakat was right for once? I enjoyed the old chauffeur Hayrullah's surprise when I summoned him to visit our main office. Apart from the meetings of the Board of Directors, which I attend on Mondays, Wednesdays and Fridays, I am not involved in the daily business of administration. Today I had a personal meeting with two bankers from Harvard (concerning the world logistics of putting three Ukrainian ballerinas on the stage). Then I made a telephone call to İz Bozok. My heart beat faster when I heard her warbling voice, 'You've stirred my journalist's instincts. I was going to ring you tomorrow anyway.' Plucking up courage, I invited her to İskele, our family restaurant, for Saturday evening and began to laugh when she answered, 'Afterwards will you show me your father's books instead of his stamp collection?' I thought to myself that if Dalga heard her she would comment, 'My dear Arda, this girl will certainly give in to you at the first opportunity.'

As soon as he picked up the phone Chief Commissioner Kasnak belched, then was silent as though waiting for me to say 'I beg your pardon.' I let him know I wished to enrol at the shooting range for practice at the end of June, and 'yes', I wanted a receipt and 'no', I hadn't given up the search for my father's killer.

(I myself don't know what I'm escaping from, and I'm hiding from myself just what I'm looking for.)

◌

I knew how touched the waiters at İskele would be when they saw me there with a woman, but I didn't expect them to be so attentive in their efforts to impress my girlfriend. With the help of white wine I began to tell my story, curious to know what her attitude would be towards me. I poured out my *inner* life in detail, but for the time being, from all those pages that resembled a detective story, I omitted completely the paragraph about losing my first love to my father. I relaxed as I talked, and İz listened wide-eyed.

I remember her saying, 'Life doesn't differentiate between the real and the imaginary, it's the children who pay the penalty for conflict between two intelligent human beings.'

As I was paying the bill I noticed Jale giggling with her snobbish friends three tables away. (Are your ears ringing, Adil Kasnak, my future Hodja?) İz noticed my expression changing.

'What's up, have they multiplied the bill instead of adding it up?' she quipped.

'In this case the problem's beyond mathematics; you won't believe it but just a few steps away is my former fiancée …'

'Hmm, a cinematic situation … I can help you in two ways. I can either pray or hold your hand so you won't be humiliated when we pass their table.'

'I certainly need both,' I said and clutching her left hand, headed for the exit with a silent prayer, aware of the mural of fish still grinning after fifteen years. Thanks to the spring chill I clung more tightly to İz's hand and we walked along Çengelköy like awkward lovers until we reached Hayrullah dozing in his ancient vehicle.

Unused to guests, İfakat brought coffee at the wrong moment; and when she took İz on a hasty tour of the mansion, she was as nervous as an officer taking his superiors round on a dormitory inspection. Our guest's only remark was, 'Would it be disrespectful if I said the place had the atmosphere of a haunted house or a chic collection of *objets d'art*?'

In the library I quickly withdrew my hand as it stretched towards the collection of my father's musical compositions. (Fearing she might fall in love with his soul I took refuge by pulling out instead the CD of Renée Fleming where I had first discovered 'Songs My Mother Taught Me'.)

She read aloud a note my father had made in a book

called *A Hittite Glossary*.[1] 'If I can't write about something from this library I'll go mad,' she said.

From her shoulder bag, embroidered with birds, she produced a notebook and I began to watch my energetic guest as she listed rare handwritten books and books from the earliest period of the printing press. Her face hadn't that blinding beauty that turns heads but was illuminated by an inner light. And her strong personality and mischievous manner were enough to cast a spell over me.

Collecting the material for the article she was planning to write, she delighted me by informing me that she would like to return on Monday morning with a photographer.

She wanted to go home sooner than I expected.

'It was a really interesting evening and I didn't feel in the least awkward at being alone with a man,' she said as she left.

I recalled that when Hayrullah had invited her to enter his cab, suspicious of an interloper, I hadn't even asked her she lived.

'Arda, something tells me this nice girl is going to bring some colour to the place,' İfakat said after she'd left.

I just managed to refrain from replying, 'Don't you know there's no happiness for me in this world?'

Still, I went to bed with a book called *Conversations*

---

1   It is thought-provoking to consider Shakespeare as the planet's most important writer of the last 450 years, when he was influenced by Homer who lived 2,300 years earlier …

with the Mediterranean Medlar Tree, in which Hikmet Birand had poured his heart out describing a rare tree:

> On the peak of Mt Çal behind Dikmen grows an old Mediterranean medlar tree. A tree where the vows of so many simple longings hang on dry branches along with the faded red and green prayer rags. I love that tree.

I was overwhelmed by the desert wind that blew through the words. (And to marry İz on Mt Çal with Hikmet Birand and the medlar tree as witnesses, and leap awake with the midday ezan floating from the city mosques.) I didn't get up until I'd finished the book. I was curious to know in what year we had lost this pastoral writer. I must find Selçuk Altun again. He had given the book to my father as a present the month he was killed.

'Since you're consulting me instead of the internet, you obviously want to know much more about Hikmet Birand than the date of his death in 1972,' he said sardonically. 'He was a close friend of the celebrated critic Nurullah Ataç and also my wife's great-uncle.'

I swore never to call this arrogant man again.

Opening the old door to the balcony, I cast a quick eye over the garden, to see if it was ready for İz's inspection next morning. May was here but again I forgot to welcome the carpet of spring growth. (At one time in my life the strange garden my mother watered even when it rained had been my confidante.) I'd go down to the garden as a slight breeze wafted the mysterious smell of the wild olive tree to my nostrils, branch by branch, like breaking waves driven to land by an offshore breeze. According to my father the overbearing Japanese persimmon tree was by itself enough to destroy a garden. My father found the atmosphere of this well-kept garden artificial, so we used to walk to Alemdağ Avenue to absorb the spring.

I drank a glass of grapefruit juice from the breakfast table and went down to the neighbouring avenue. I passed the market's resident pretzel-seller, with a word, 'If you don't ask how many lira to the dollar I'll buy a pretzel-roll,' and turned into Alemdağ. (At the first bite my pretzel fell to the ground and I imagined my mother scolding me from heaven.) Should I walk faster? Every step took me back twelve years, month by month, square by square. The denser the traffic the more and more exotic became the aroma of the wild olive trees that poured into the avenue. My father loved the clumps of shameless weeds and nameless flowers multiplying in the old wall's embrace, and saw their function as 'a healer in the tunnel of time'. I dived into a garden of debris, a dodgy inheritance whose owner had fled to Buenos Aires. Behind the garden was a graffitied wall, left over from the '60s: my father would say, 'It's not funny but I feel like laughing.'

I sheltered in the shade of a dwarf plum tree by a dry well which had frightened me in my childhood, and at the sound of the afternoon ezan I dozed off.

CR

Long live Kuzguncuk! I had always thought it was a quiet district that had sheltered Ottoman refugees fleeing from the Balkans. If my father had gone along İcadiye Street, which leads headlong down to the sea, he might have said, 'The market has a rural atmosphere with its boxy stalls radiating from a central hub.' I had no difficulty in finding Bereketli Street that led into the Avenue, and as I walked among the attractive wooden houses I was as excited as though I'd got lost in the midst of a miniature city. I had a bunch of flowers in my hand – I didn't know what kind – and a packet of almond paste bought specially by İfakat. Climbing upstairs to the third floor of the apartment block called İnşirah, I knew I was about to learn the meaning of that name.

And, wearing kitchen gloves, İz opened the door and said, 'Welcome to the building of *inner comfort.*' The geometrically patterned kilim, a non-figurative sketch and a map signed Heritiers de Homann on the wall seemed to demonstrate the way two people who share a house can live in awkward togetherness. Zuhâl, who wore John Lennon spectacles and edited the 'city-life' section of a competing newspaper, had proudly hung the antique map that included her birthplace Tirebolu (Tripoli) on the wall. While the hosts were preparing savoury pancakes in the kitchen, her swarthy boyfriend, Zafer, with oily hair dangling from both sides of a head that seemed too small for his square-shaped body, was shooting a line about his degrees in economics and sociology from a minor university in Florida. I was warming to this fellow who taught sociology in a state university, but mainly supported himself with the rent he collected from two shops inherited from his aunt.

I'm used to being stared at sometimes like a panda in a zoo, because of my Viking-like features. Uneasy with the three soulmates who watched me as though they were counting my every bite, I eventually dropped my wineglass. I noticed İz was pleased when she found some way to console me. Zafer was busy announcing that his bookworm girlfriend hadn't read anything after Dostoevsky, much to Zuhâl's delicious embarrassment. (I recalled my father's sympathy for the repulsive Selçuk Altun's refusal to read any novel before Kafka.) Just before the male and female Z's left for a 'get well' visit to the latter's aunt, the former leaned over and whispered in my ear, 'We're going to get along just fine, brother-in-law.'

I wonder why this gave me an erection.

At the end of a noisy folk song tape, İz brought in the draft of an article she'd prepared on my father and his library. After twice reading the fourth paragraph about his ability to multiply five-digit numbers in his head at the speed of a computer, I couldn't resist multiplying two six-digit numbers in my head, three times in a row, refereed by a minute Citizen calculator. She was far more surprised than I expected. Galvanized by Dalga's cheers from the upper stands in the clouds, I leant over towards İz's lips.

ᘓ

On the title page of Melina Mercouri's autobiography, my father had jotted down, 'Beware the day when a nostalgic chorus line, an old aphorism or a line of lyrical poetry fails to ignite the joy of life.' I had scratched out the note and added, when mother was taken to hospital, 'No problem, if you have Ada Ergenekon as the chief firefighter in your life!' Before calling İz, who never wasted words, I had to take time to prepare myself for a salvo of sharp comments. We used to either meet three or four times a week or speak on the phone twice a day. In our marathons through the back streets of medieval Beyoğlu and Üsküdar, how genuinely she loved those sunbaked urchins. I thought she bought lottery tickets just to be able to say to the itinerant vendors who usually sought out the shadiest corners of local parks, 'Can I pay when I win?' We would eat at makeshift diners and rundown hotel restaurants, giggling all the time. Anyone watching us might have thought I was urging this strange girl to talk non-stop as therapy. (God forbid!) On the contrary, when she spoke I felt myself relax. I would listen to her, hungry like someone who has endured a decade of solitude and longing on a desert island, or passionately, like someone listening to a rhapsody of new delights. She was amused at my embarrassment when she leaned over to ask for a cigarette from the next table, or when she was served her Turkish coffee in a tea glass. When I dared to look into her dark eyes my heart warmed, but I was always aware of feeling that that might cause the light in her eyes to fade.

Although I was only seven months younger, I was pleased at first that she acted as if she was my older sister. I realized that she was trying to look out for me, assuming I found it hard to deal with life's difficulties. (It wasn't easy to shake off my paranoid suspicion I was being tested by this guardian angel, who was rather like a happy medium between my mother and Dalga, both of whom I had lost.) When we went out to eat with her friends she watched me from the corner of her eye while she was talking to others and I would feel uneasy. İz had an interesting group of friends who regarded her as leader. Most of them were getting by with jobs that didn't interest them in order to pursue their real passions which no one respected. I knew I would be accused by the Harvard crowd of being a turncoat, mixing with a bunch that consisted of a poet (translator), a painter (teacher of foreign languages), an art historian (tourist guide), an assistant theatre director (film dubbing work), an industrial designer (proofreader) and those who found themselves working in the media sector without an education in communications.

In the shady cafés and piss-stinking jazz bars of Beyoğlu and Bağdat Street, İz made fun of the pseudo-intellectuals who sneered at the simple mistakes made by others. I had sympathy for the identical twins Beste and Güfte, flute and cello honours graduates from the conservatoire. Although they often teased me, I derived great pleasure from observing the ongoing exchange of insults between the two chubby girls who edited competing magazines. On the thirteenth of every month we all met for dinner at the fashionable Ottoman restaurant Hünkâr, in Nişantaş. Everyone had to show up unless they had a good excuse. The Ügümü brothers assumed that the group of twenty friends was the country's élite media team, and respectfully allocated the top floor of the restaurant to the nihilist bunch.

The incident happened on the second Hünkâr campaign. Apparently I had incurred a penalty for failing to acknowledge the 775th anniversary of the Ulucami monument in Divriği:

'He should at least sing a folksong halfway through …'

'What if I recite a poem of Küçük İskender's?'

'He should spend a night with Beste and Güfte in the same bed …'

'What if I paid for all your dinners for a whole year?'

'He should tell us an impromptu story,' Azmi the art critic and sculptor proposed. I was astonished to hear İz supporting the suggestion but saying, 'And please, no happy ending.' When our eyes met, I felt she sensed the secret I was keeping from her, almost as if she wanted me to reveal it in code. When she saw me hesitating, she stroked my hair and commanded, 'Finish your drink and then please start, dear Arda.'

As I finished my drink I recalled Küçük İskender's quip, 'I have to plan and commit a murder within an hour and it has been troubling me for minutes.' I began with a prayer.

'Once upon a time there was a wealthy lady called Adalet Ergin who lived in Istanbul, where heaven and hell mingle. By the beloved Bosphorus, in the waterside mansion she inherited from her first husband who died of a heart attack, she lived happily with her second husband Rasim, her eighteen-year-old daughter Deniz from her first marriage, and her eleven-year-old son Aras from the second. The handsome Rasim had once been the finance director of the cotton-thread factory in the suburb of Haramidere. It had been left to his wife by her first husband. (The children don't know that the fiancée from whom he had separated to marry his Adalet had committed suicide. He took his wife's family name and rose to become vice-chairman of the firm's board of directors.)

'It seems Adalet was pleased that Deniz, encouraged by Rasim, had taken up basketball and risen to the national junior team, and that she had accepted her stepfather and was devoted to her brother. Aras was a very talented and sensitive child, who appeared to be the apple of his family's eye. He never left his mother's side from the moment he learned to stand up and grab her skirt. He would cry his eyes out if he couldn't join Adalet in the toilet, and he couldn't even listen to a story and take his afternoon nap unless his mother scratched his back. Once a week he would make her read the story of "The Little Match

Girl" who froze to death on the street selling matches on Christmas night, and in tears he would say, "But Mother, surely the Little Match Girl went to heaven?" Neither of his parents nor any of his teachers ever had to raise their voice to this mature and well-behaved boy. It's said that his mother sacked the Welsh nanny when she claimed, "Aras will have psychological problems in the future because he has never fully lived his childhood." By the time he finished primary school he was listening to classical music, and his violin teacher swore he played Vivaldi almost like a virtuoso.

'Aras began to enjoy accompanying his father to Deniz's basketball matches, and also to Fenerbahçe football matches. The second big secret he kept from his mother was that he ate fried meatballs, traditional street food, before he entered the stadium. The first match he went to watch his sister play in, he felt hundreds of pairs of eyes feeding on her long and shapely legs. He cried when his father laughed at his suggestion that "Deniz should play in a tracksuit." Adalet was also not informed about the father and son's monthly outings to the Golden Horn. As soon as they lowered their fancy fishing-rods off the Atatürk Bridge, Rasim began to tell his son about his dissolute adventures chasing after women. Aras would always listen eagerly to his father's fantasy, in which he dressed up as a woman, entered a dormitory for girl students and made love to the three roommates till morning. Then they would walk to modest, quiet Kıztaşı and stop over at Rasim's mother's house. Aras could never understand why his mother had forbidden him to see the grandmother with the grey-blue eyes and her blind daughter, his aunt. Aunt Ruzin would move her hands slo…w…ly over his face and touch him as if wondering who he resembled. Rasim would pretend not to have heard her when his twin sister asked, "Aras, which is more painful, do you think, to lose your personality or lose your eyes?"

'In his first year of primary school Aras gets roughed up by a boy two years older. Rasim raids the bully's home, beats up his father and big brother and destroys the furniture in their living room. The neighbourhood hooligans avoid Aras, afraid of Deniz's skill in karate, and Aras wonders if all his talents are a kind of punishment. Out of loneliness he takes refuge in books and music, and when asked what he'd like as an award for passing his primary exams with flying colours, he answers, "Permission to become a musician when I grow up, because my big sister will manage your business better than me."

'A supreme inconvenience was inflicted on millions of Istanbul citizens in the name of security, when the President of the USA and the heads of state of forty-five other countries assembled for NATO's umpteenth summit meeting. The same night it ended was also the night drunk Rasim crashed his Jaguar into a battered old minibus. He got away with minor scratches and was able to bury the incident, while Adalet was to spend a considerable time in intensive care and Aras, neglected by his father and sister, fell into a depression. He looked out from his balcony over the restless waves of the Bosphorus and slipped away into periods of d...ee...p sleep holding Sara, his yellow-haired cat. A week after the accident, on the night when the Olympic torch passed through the city's busy streets – closed to traffic right in the middle of the rush hour – his sister sent Aras with their driver Nurullah to see *Spiderman 2*. But Aras came back without seeing the second half of the film. On the way up to his room he heard moans from his mother's bedroom and rushed in to see his father and stepsister making passionate love on his mother's bed. He was shocked! Silently he ran to Nurullah's house in the back garden and sobbed out what he had seen. Then he went up to his room. Shaking all over, clasping Sara, he threw himself into the relentless waters of the Bosphorus. The corpse of Aras still holding Sara tight hit the shore somewhere near the Bebek Mosque.

'Two weeks later, Adalet was discharged from hospital, but broke down when she heard from Nurullah what had happened. Her hair turned white. First she threw Deniz out. She paid her daughter's university fees to study psychology in England, but cut her off and said she never wanted to see her again. Rasim refused to agree to a divorce. He insisted moreover that if he was denied an immediate payment of $10 million, he would turn over all the company's undeclared transactions to the Treasury. Nurullah shot Rasim through the heart with a single bullet from his own gun. The death report appeared as "suicide due to depression".

'Adalet, a resilient woman, was not altogether cut off from life. She gave herself to religion and charitable causes, but whenever she heard the sound of a violin she broke down completely, beating her breast and crying, "My son, my only son … I'm suffering in this hell; I'm not worthy to be near you in paradise, my beloved son."'

Three apples are said to fall from the sky: one for the story-teller, one for the listeners and the last for the one who understands …

&

I knew that this invented tragedy would boost respect for me in the eyes of İz. We began to go on weekend trips together, spending many nights in desolate hotels in medieval towns, where I memorized every inch of her body. We visited towns hundreds of kilometres from Istanbul, where humanity prevails and where there are eating houses that offer delectable meals for the equivalent of $5. In the legendary national park of Kazdağı, many attractive villages of houses built with cut stone blocks were almost empty. While villagers crowded to Istanbul to look for work, the young generation in Istanbul had been taking over these monumental stone houses one by one. We had covered every inch of the tired old forests of dramatic Kazdağı. If I came face to face again with the pomegranate and almond trees, the mulberry and honeysuckle bushes protected by the pine forest, I would probably not recognize them, nor birds like the Bosphorus shearwater, the bee bird, the chaffinch, the black-headed bunting or, for that matter, the greenfinch. But I remember distinctly how we fell asleep in each other's arms among the poppies that surrounded the meadows. I don't think I'll ever again see the souvenir shops with their absurd signs, or the sulky tea-house waiters who refused tips.

İz's parents, who never once stopped arguing, had come to Istanbul for a family wedding. As her mother looked me up and down suspiciously, I tried to convey with my eyes, 'Calm down, silly woman, I've no intention of becoming your son-in-law.'

I knew İz and my uncle would like each other. He invited us to his favourite restaurant and produced a small bag in which there were thirty-two news cuttings from 2003. He asked me to pick ten for him to examine and serve up as an absurd novel.

1. Kütahya: When they thought the laser show at the opening of the Z Bar was a UFO they banned laser shows the following year.

2. Samsun: M.P. (22) robbed the local branch of a bank and was caught two months later trying to deposit money at the same branch.

3. Bursa: S.K. (30) shot all the tomatoes when he learned

there were no green peppers left in the greengrocer's. 'What kind of greengrocer is this?' he asked.

4. Adana: The Association for the Protection of Domestic Poultry was busted for organizing cockfights.

5. Bursa: A mosque holding 3,000 people was built in C., a town of 3,000 people.

6. Paris: The Turk who threw his camera on the pitch at the Turkey – Brazil football friendly was identified by the police when they developed the film in his camera.

7. Adapazarı: S.A., the health officer in the Accident and Emergency department of a state hospital, left his place for two hours to a retired mariner, C.V.; a doctor caught the mariner giving stitches to a patient who had cut his hand.

8. Sivas: A.K., dreaming that his wife Ş. was having an affair, killed her in front of her children by cutting her throat.

9. Aydın: Thinking his wife had gone out, M.G. (28) brought his lover back in the boot of his car. Realizing his wife was at home he forgot all about the lover, who

was later rescued by the police when they heard banging from the boot.

10. Bursa: Intoxicated L.A. parked her car on a downhill slope, but instead of putting on the handbrake she lay down in front of the car.

೧

I went to the shooting range because I had made a promise to Adil Kasnak and I wanted an excuse to have my registration deleted at the earliest opportunity. That would give me the chance to enjoy some poetic insults from the man shaped like a polar bear. When he asked, 'Do you really want a receipt?' I recalled a newspaper report on how 'In the Turkish economy 66 out of every 100 lira goes unrecorded,' and how '114 different ways to evade tax have been discovered.'

'Encouraging your customers in tax evasion doesn't look good, Mr Adil,' I said.

'Don't be so pompous, my boy, like some youngster who's just stopped wanking and started going to knocking-shops. You must know that this is how the market tries to survive. I apologize for assuming that you might use the tax you've saved for better things than the government ...'

We entered the shooting range together. The place wasn't as primitive as I expected. A dozen heavyweight men with goggles and earplugs were running around like waddling ducks, taking cover behind obstacles, appearing to practise shooting, sometimes single-handed and sideways, at times with both hands, standing up or squatting.

The chaotic improvisation came to an end when the trainer in the red trousers and purple t-shirt blew his whistle. The pupils gathered dutifully round him in a half-circle. I wasn't surprised to hear complaints when they were required to fire six shots in twelve seconds.

'I could never work with this team,' I told Adil.

'I thought you might say that, Ergenekon Junior, but if you pay the difference I can arrange for you to take one-to-one lessons from the best shooting coach in the city ...'

So I was going to meet Cahid Çiftçi, who was to have more influence on me than any of my Harvard tutors. Adil Kasnak had added, 'One of his eccentricities is to get annoyed when people pronounce the last letter of his name as "t". He is from Eastern Anatolia. His wife died giving birth to twins, who also died. He never remarried. He was a truck driver, but was forced to retire early after a road accident left him with permanent damage to his foot. Before that he must have been the best hunter in the Istranca Mountains. When you get used to his ugly mug you'll realize what an interesting fellow he is, my boy ...'

Cahid didn't look older than forty-five though he had thick ash-coloured hair. He had this depressed look as though he might burst into tears if you asked, 'How are you?' I thought for a moment he reminded me of Lennie, the naive giant in *Of Mice and Men*. The tides of a deep and noble loneliness were hidden in his eyes. I was expecting Kasnak to scratch his balls, appreciating that we were two of a kind. Cahid Hodja screwed up his face every time he put weight on his lame foot, then looked relieved as though his punishment lessened at each step. I had to work on him for two sessions to stop him addressing me as 'Sir'.

During training he threw off his haunted look and roared like a fanatical preacher, showing as much respect for the guns as though they were thoroughbred mares. Somehow he spotted in me the talent of a 'sharpshooter'. (It seems that I'm at one with the gun as if it were part of my body, and my arm forms a natural extension to the grip.) Apparently if the weapon doesn't receive bodily warmth it transmits its own coldness of soul back to the body. Consequently, to be 'integrated' with the metallic texture, I was confined for ten days to a Webley brand, 'single-shot' antique revolver. As I grasped the long-handled weapon with both hands and focused on the huge mirror, I recalled a documentary scene of copulating turtles.

On the way to work I would carry this antique gun in my bag, and at home when I went to bed I would hide it under my pillow and pray. The ritual I tolerated for Cahid Hodja's sake was complete when I finally ate the blessed sugar cubes. I imagined my enigmatic Hodja would eventually make me a present of a minimalist Webley.

Cahid Çiftçi's theatrical teaching technique encouraged me. I would feel like grabbing a machinegun and maniacally firing at all the target stands when I heard him say, 'Well done, you monster, good for you.'

He would say, 'Draw a virtual line between your right eye and the target, then let the bullets fly like fury along that line.' I could never have imagined that I would be more relaxed at the shooting range than at the swankiest spa. I was happy to join the ranks of the advanced students. On the eighth week, Kasnak had watched my successful performance shooting at a distance of twenty-five and fifty metres. I managed to make him admit, 'You focus on the target like a born sniper and you caress the trigger as if you're counting prayer beads. Well done!'

Once a week I took Cahid to local restaurants where he chose to read a liberal newspaper, or the colossal *Turkish Dictionary*. I confess I enjoyed watching him looking around suspiciously at the local traders smacking their lips and bolting a quick lunch. Every time he brought the fork to his mouth the sight of him finishing another bite under stress was as impressive as a dervish dance. But to make him sweat from embarrassment I would call İz and exchange erotic chat while we waited for our coffees. He was a good listener in spite of his sorrowful eyes that seemed to say, 'Don't even try to ask me any personal questions.'

The night of 11 July, when İz left for Adapazarı[1] to

---

1   In nearby Adapazarı in the second week of July, millions of white butterflies reproduce in the white poplars, deposit their larvae and set off on their last flight over the river Sakarya to die. A dense cloud like falling snow covers the Sakarya Bridge and holds up the traffic.

witness nature's tragedy, I forced Cahid Çiftçi to come
to the İskele Restaurant. Bit by bit I told my Hodja my
whole life story. All I learned about him was that he lived
in modest Ümraniye, on the second floor of an apartment
block. If I did start to look for my father's killer now, I had
an accomplished guide who knew how to keep his mouth
shut.

From the day I met İz I never had nightmares, except
for one in which I made clammy love with my beloved's
housemate, Zuhâl, who had had her large breasts cut off,
like the woman in one of Küçük İskender's poems. As soon
as I kissed İz I was completely at peace with my life. I had
met her with the help of the repulsive Selçuk Altun and
for this reason I feared the surprise second act of the play.

രൂ

Uncle Salvador fell in love with the tender young girl in
a painting by Herbert Draper, which he bought from a
London gallery. The nude with the angelic face in the
picture he named Sylvie. Her profile, as she reached out
to clasp a 200-year-old strand of seaweed, reminded me
of Alexander the Great. My uncle set off on a tour to
write an absurd novel. The day he returned to Istanbul he
called me excitedly. 'I could be reaching a turning point in
my life, dear Arda,' he said. 'The captivating girl having
anal sex with a one-armed black man on a Dutch-made
video that I've watched three times is the spitting image

of Sylvie! I'm taking the first flight to Amsterdam and I'm not coming back till I find her.'

'If you're proposing to marry this porn star I hope you won't claim back the bonds and real estate you passed over to me, because I may not give them back,' I said. Since I had begun to shoot bullets like peanuts I'd become edgy and stubborn.

The morning my uncle shot off to Amsterdam a letter arrived at my office address, written on the back of a supermarket receipt and marked 'Personal'. Inside a crumpled envelope was written:

SON OF A TURNCOAT JEWISH BITCH! NOW YOUR LIFE IS GOING TO BE A PRISON, EFFEMINATE FAGGOT! WAIT FOR YOUR DEMON FROM HELL …

Assuming it was a joke by Beste and Güfte, I put the message and its envelope in my jacket pocket and concentrated on my series of meetings. As I set out at night for the shooting range, I felt every particle in my body quiver with paranoia. Surely the teasing twins wouldn't play such a shallow trick? I had never harmed anyone but myself in my entire life, so why was my life to be made a prison? I didn't think my parents had left any unpaid bills. I began to wonder about this threat that so completely missed the mark, from someone unaware that for me imprisoned life would actually be a form of reward.

Annoyed with my bad performance, Cahid Hodja left me alone for a while. The more I pulled the trigger as an act of therapy the more my hands shook. The Hodja returned to me after ten minutes and for the first and last time put his left hand on my shoulder. I can hardly describe how relieved I was to hear him say, 'I'm ready to forget this session. Your finger won't jump to the trigger unless you're ready, and Arda, you only lose a gun's respect once.'

I didn't mention the note to İz. Two days later I had even forgotten where I'd put it.

On the night of 22 July I dropped İz off and drove home alone. It was the night when six carriages of the Ankara express came off the rails. At first the official number of dead announced was 139, later the figure dropped to 37. The academicians had warned of the weak infrastructure and of the fatal danger it posed if it continued to travel. But those responsible for the calamity refused to resign. I was wandering along the main street which even the stray dogs avoided, and was listening in distress to Pat Metheny. I was trying to find some relief by cursing all those mustachioed men who shared responsibility for the train accident. Though I was intoxicated, I noticed a shadow jumping in front of the car. If I hadn't been cruising slowly my jeep would have thrown him all the way to the Ottoman cemetery. (I shouldn't have stopped under the dim street lamp.) I recognized the stout man reeking of rakı who grinned and suddenly flashed a flick-knife under my chin. Seydo, whom my mother had had beaten up, his shop destroyed and his family chased from Çamlıca for calling me 'son of a turncoat Jewish bitch', was now back fifteen years later saying, 'It's me again, you son of a turncoat Jew!'

With a sudden blow to my face he pulled me out of the car and began to drag me towards the seaside cemetery.

'If you try to yell, I'll carve you up in the middle of the street!'

I shuddered, remembering that I'd read that in our country a crime is committed every two minutes, and that 32.7 per cent of cases that reach the courts remain unresolved. I wasn't expecting to see an empty police box on this dead-end street I had turned into for the second time in my life. Seydo continued his harangue until we reached the point where this squat box like an igloo was illuminated.

'When your creepy-crawly mother threw us out of our place, my father's business was ruined. When he died of a heart attack, my uncle made my mother marry an elderly widower. I never heard from my little sister again after that bastard sent her to the south to become another octogenarian's second wife. Then the week I came back from my military service the stingy scoundrel kicked me out of the house. As if prison in Istanbul wasn't enough, I moved from prison to prison in Anatolia. What I never got from school and family, I got from a heavy-duty convict from Diyarbakır who took me under his wing. I was released after an amnesty and then I started to make more money than the president.

'When I came back to Istanbul from my final underworld mission abroad, I learned that the angel Azrael had already taken the lives of my stepfather and your creepy mother,' he ended.

I had to lean against the police booth, retracting every time he prodded my throat with the flick-knife. I felt waves of fire spread through my body as he slapped me repeatedly across the face. My eyes were glued to the memorial stones in the Ottoman cemetery opposite. I thought his eyes grew bigger in the moonlight and were as eerie as my revengeful mother's. I was even more frightened when he said, 'You haven't committed a crime that requires me to kill you. I don't know if this is a reward or a punishment but just to torment your mother's soul, I'm going to rape your right here, Jewish bastard!'

What wouldn't I have given for a gun in my hand! At the command 'Give over!' it was as if a blessed hand pressed the button of an anti-fly spray twice and Seydo collapsed like a clumsy sack. I remembered from the novels of Erje Ayden the poetic sound of a gun with a silencer. As the sound of rhythmic footsteps retreated, running through the cemetery and splitting the silence of the night, I crumpled up like a helpless kitten. My body was trembling and I felt my heart would stop. Noticing Seydo's still erect tool sticking out of his open zipper I began to vomit.

As soon as I recovered I picked myself up and tried to run to the jeep, but I could only walk by clinging to the chalky wall of the cemetery. It wouldn't have surprised me if my mother had made an agreement with a gang of trigger-happy gunmen to keep me under surveillance even after she died. I wondered how often I would be mugged and what part of my body would suffer in reprisal for her lunacies.

On my safe return home my heart began to revive, as if I had lived through the joyful shock of an unexpected release from an endless prison sentence. When I kissed İfakat's cheek at midnight as she was washing up, she asked, 'So have you proposed to İz?' I took one and a half sleeping pills when I went to bed and hoped to God I'd forget everything I'd suffered in the last two hours and that this would be the very last page in my anthology of nightmares.

I leapt up with the morning ezan and after a long thoughtful shower I dressed in my darkest suit and made for the seaside cemetery. At every step my heart beat faster. It was startling not to see Seydo's body on the slope down to the police box; if I hadn't seen my own vomit strewn with apricot skins, I could have sworn that I had dreamt last night. I shivered with relief and walked towards the market, tracing the bare tombstones of those Ottoman soldiers, doctors and higher civil servants who died young. I knew I'd come on our neighbourhood pretzel seller at the lonely park gate, reading a tabloid aloud.

'If you don't ask me anything about dervishes, I'll buy two pretzel-rolls.'

But I was a bit ashamed when he replied, as he arranged his wares, 'Did they send you to America to end up talking like that after ten years? Who can we ask, Mr Arda, if not you?'

I went to my office with unusual zeal. While I'd been fighting for my life my unmonitored email address was contacted at least twice. The first was from the repulsive Selçuk Altun:

Dear Arda,

I hope it's a good sign, but last night I dreamt you were lying face-down by a graveyard, crying for help. Before I could reach you, you got up and thanked a shadow, ran off and jumped into the Bosphorus ... I send you my best wishes and hope we can meet soon to talk. Love to İz ...

Then my irrepressible uncle:

Arda, Arda, Arda,

I wish I'd never found Sylvie's imaginary sister! Demi is a bisexual transvestite who's had the operation, but is still a friend to Turks. (She'll be my guest next summer.) You'd probably be angry if you read in one of my stories that her boyfriend and girlfriend were each other's cousins. I found Cornell Woolrich's 1930 book, A Young Man's Heart, *in the secondhand bookshop run by her man Vin. I'm flying to*

San Francisco to follow up Helen M. Grady, owner of the
book in 1931. An experimental novel in which Demi and
Helen's paths will cross …

he went on bullshitting. The unruly Salvador's attempts to
carry out research for his writings were always unsuccessful,
while I, unbeknownst to him, lived real detective stories.

☙

In the restful restaurant of the mysterious Four Seasons
Hotel, where I was meeting a babbling banker for dinner,
I heard news that turned my blood to ice. İz had been in
some kind of a traffic accident and had been taken to the
intensive care unit of a private hospital on the Asiatic side
of the city. Was this the staging of the bloody final act in
which I would lose her? (My whole being rose in torment.)
I rushed to the Lokman Hospital. What if I were to lose
İz? Could I ever connect with life again?

I found Zuhâl in the soulless waiting room of the
intensive care unit. She was still in shock. 'We had just seen
a Nicole Kidman film and were on our way home in İz's
Suzuki. We noticed that a shop in İcadiye Street was open
and we stopped for a soft drink. I got out first. Suddenly a
Land Cruiser the size of a tank crashed into the jeep from
the rear and threw her down just as she was loosening her
safety belt. It was awful. I think I saw İz's head coming
through the windscreen and then the giant jeep tore away
with arabesque music pouring from the open windows. İz

has had a cerebral haemorrhage and there are hundreds of tiny glass fragments stuck in her face …' and she burst into tears again.

The doctor on duty, of the gold Rolex watch, then spoke, 'Your friend has had a concussion of medium intensity. Once we've checked the level of blood-accumulation in the head we can operate, though we'll have to wait forty-eight hours before we do so. The operation should be a success, all being well. Unfortunately, though, her face is severely damaged. I know a lot of lacerated women who have seen their faces, and even though they've survived the haemorrhage, they scream, "Why did you save me?"'

My head was spinning. I was permitted to go in for just ten minutes. I hoped the room number in the intensive care unit wasn't a message. (285. The unlucky number on my middle-school certificate!) As soon as I saw İz under the respirator I shut my eyes and began to cry. Her face was covered by a mask of minced meat over her forehead and cheeks. Bits of glass protruded from every pore, and as though that wasn't enough, her nose and lips were torn, the fragments glittering on and off like a mocking smile. I thought I'd never seen such a terrifying face even in my worst nightmares. I looked at Dr Rolex, who was completing an inventory of the damage, 'three teeth broken', and he immediately left the room. Was that the hint of a smile I saw as I tried to pull myself together and focus on İz? I remembered the traffic accident I had years ago; the bed where I lay limp as a scarecrow, how

I had felt my pain stop at last and my body grow light as a caique floating on a whitish-grey river. Hoping the path of desolation would end in a moment of peace, I too might have tried to smile. During the convalescence I had described a dream to my mother, and she had interpreted the meaning behind it: 'You seem to flirt with death, Arda; but I'm not going to hand over your life, not even to the Angel of Death, my fine son, before he takes mine.'

Apart from her bruised fingernails, painted yellow and blue in honour of the Fenerbahçe football team, my Beloved's hands were bandaged. As I pressed my lips to her right index finger I couldn't help noticing my heart warming and I was no longer disturbed by her tragic face. I remembered what Graham Greene had said to his old mistress Yvonne Cloetta, on the eve of his death, 'I've just realized that true love emerges between two people when there's no longer any sex drive.' I bent close to her ear, 'Listen, funny girl,' I said, 'you'll come out of this hospital safe and sound. The best plastic surgeons on the planet are going to restore your face to its former self, God willing. Whatever happens I'll never leave you! Perhaps we'll marry, I really don't care if you can't go out amongst people for a while, or even ever. I could even be happy because you'll have more time for me. Anyway I don't like crowds, and you will discover the secret of silence …'

I took to the doctor who was to perform the operation. He looked just like Woody Allen when he frowned. I was surprised when he didn't ask for two thirds of his fee in dollars. The owner of the shop had been giving hell to his assistant on the pavement at the time of the accident, and had given the police the licence number of the runaway car. But when the young owner of the Land Cruiser, Kutsi Serhamza, turned out to be the nephew of some minister or other and the son of a building contractor, a prominent member of a religious sect, his testimony 'disappeared'. Both İz's and Zuhâl's bosses were heavily in debt to public banks and the department for privatization, and had managed to prevent news of the accident appearing in the tabloid press. I was concentrating on İz's condition so couldn't react to the disgusting developments, but I recalled part of a poem by Küçük İskender called 'Dulcinia's Journal'.[1]

İz's friendly father, who had left with his wife for the US to welcome the birth of their grandchild, came back alone for the operation. When he saw I had taken charge of the arrangements he slipped into the background. The operation was a success. As İz's health insurance only covered 20 per cent of the hospital expenses, I paid the rest.

When, in spite of my warnings, İz looked at her face in the mirror she was overcome by screaming and tears.

---

1   What are we doing, Mustafa, what is our business here?
     On this planet, in this contemptible system, in these lands
     without character
     why are we living still in misery?
     Why are we struggling still, Mustafa?
     The police either beat us up or collude!
     If it's the state we mean …
     There are people the state reckons far more important than us.

She was to be in the hospital another seventy-two hours, to prevent the risk of chronic bleeding. I took her mother, who made it to the hospital the next day, to İz's room while she was asleep and I was glad when she fainted without screaming. Whatever the repulsive Selçuk Altun said when he phoned her to send his best wishes, her eyes tried to laugh. Later, he gave me the London address of a skilled surgeon, an expert in such cases, but upset me by saying, 'This arrogant man will perhaps accept a patient only in four months' time, but if your mother had been in charge she would have had İz on the operating table at the first opportunity.'

İz, the daughter of a retired and honest civil servant, hadn't even enough money to go on holiday. She objected when I proposed to pay for the plastic surgery, and I replied, 'Listen, funny girl. I propose we get married as soon as your face is healed, with God's help. If you become my wife, I'll deduct what you owe me from your allowances, and if you end up with someone else, I'll invoice your moronic husband ...'

İz was immensely touched by my sensitivity during this time of strife. (So was I.) But now that she no longer looked at me lovingly, as if I was her little brother, I felt a lot less confident. The surgeon recommended two weeks' rest before travelling to London. The morning of her discharge from hospital, İz let her exhausted family know she would be staying with me until we left together for the UK. She scolded her mother when she reacted as if she were going to work in a brothel. While the tiresome woman was running from the room in tears, I remembered once again that I had never been able to say 'no' to my mother, not even once.

İz was trembling when she walked out into the light of day, her face wrapped in a turquoise scarf that Zuhâl had brought. On the way home I realized stupid Hayrullah was staring at her through the rearview mirror and I cheerfully banged him on the neck with my bag. İfakat turned out to be more resilient than I thought. When she embraced İz and said, 'May God swiftly take the life of whoever left your lovely face in this state,' was this a divine message? (Wouldn't any servant of God take this Kutsi demon's life for $50,000, or a chosen servant like Cahid, for $100,000? But first I had to soothe the pain of my İz of the beautiful soul ...)

One evening after the ezan İz had another fit of crying. Sending her to sleep with the aid of sleeping pills, I remained sleepless, and as though under a spell I began to read the first novel Selçuk Altun had signed for my mother. I thought the title *Loneliness Comes from the Road You Go Down*, borrowed from the poet Oktay Rifat, was a manoeuvre to increase the sales of the book. I didn't go to sleep until I had finished it. The following day I read his other two novels, both of them at one go. I knew now why my mother hadn't steered me towards these works which, I had to admit, were absorbing. Unfortunately this unattractive man, whom I had known since childhood, had

– when in trouble – used me as a model for the protagonist and narrator in his novels. (I really can't say I have any more sympathy for him than for my father's murderer.)

My uncle, who came back empty-handed from San Francisco, announced, 'The city was too humid even for masturbating.' (I knew he would ignore the pain İz was suffering.) The next day we took off for London with high hopes. Of her group, İz had allowed only Zuhâl to come to the airport and, wrapped in her scarf, she was tense as if all eyes were on her. We collected our boarding cards and settled in the most out-of-the-way café we could find. While she was engrossed in a feminist comic book, Zuhâl leaned over and whispered, 'Don't let her know, but I'm convinced that lout Kutsi Serhamza is sitting three tables behind.' I turned round with a shudder of loathing as if a rattlesnake was behind me. The stocky, mongoloid-looking rascal in a Versace shirt was on his feet putting out his cigarette with clumsy fingers. The gorilla on steroids who was attentively holding his case and mobile phone must have been his personal bodyguard. He lurched away towards his hell, his waddling walk imitating ex-president Turgut Özal. I cursed this swaggering hypocrite behind his back as he strutted off. Inspired like an elephant who remembers forty years later who shot down his mate, I committed every inch of him to memory.

Following a series of delay announcements at half-hourly intervals, we eventually boarded the plane. The stewardess in business class peered at İz to a most annoying degree.

As soon as İz swallowed her pill, she sank into a deep sleep. I covered her entire face with the scarf, except for her nostrils and mouth, and wrapped her closely in a blanket. (I notice I'm getting used to such things.) Before I started to read Haruki Murakami's *Sputnik Sweetheart*, just like one of Selçuk Altun's odd heroes, I looked at sublime Istanbul; those who failed to win her soul have now raped her body stone by stone.

ᘓ

This was İz's first visit to London, and she was intently examining everything around her. We settled down in the Ritz Hotel next to Le Meridien where Dalga had staged her confessional. I had a premonition that we would be shown to the gloomy room 423, where Graham Greene and Selçuk Altun's paranoid character Sina had stayed.

Next day, around noon, we went fearfully to Dr Rohatgi's private office in Harley Street. The receptionist, who looked like a retired model, immediately ushered us into a claustrophobic room. There were eight cell-like cubicles into which the patients retreated to prevent them alarming one other. Pam almost had a fit when she realized that we had turned up without an appointment.

Apparently at that moment the doctor was phoning his assistant in Boston. I covertly slipped a £50 note into Pam's pocket. 'I take all the responsibility, please don't try to stop

me,' I said and dived into the doctor's room. I was startled
when the Indian, who faced the wall behind him, and
spoke on the phone with an accented but poetic English,
suddenly turned round at the sound of the door opening. I
don't ever recall seeing such an ugly man before in my life.
(I couldn't help wondering which part of his body didn't
require plastic surgery.) I prepared to be kicked out of the
room when he started to scan me with his bulging eyes,
but with a smile he signalled to me to sit in the armchair
closest to his table and turned back to the wall to continue
his conversation. According to his business card on the
table, he had graduated from Oxford University Medical
School in 1979. I sighed, wondering whether my mother,
if she had seen the degrees after his name, BMBch,
BA(Hons), FRCS(Eng), DM, FRCS(Plast) while I was
in high school, would have wanted me to become a plastic
surgeon. I counted the busts of fourteen sulky-faced
composers standing on mahogany pedestals dotted around
his office.

He finished his conversation, and a familiar piano tune
gradually filled the room.

'Are you Eidur Gudjohnsen or his twin brother?' he
asked.

I wondered uncomfortably if I should feel happy to
end up with a Chelsea-supporter surgeon, immediately
emphasizing that I was a Harvard graduate. I summarized
dramatically the events of the previous week.

'I still can't believe that I'm looking at a Turk with the

154

physique of a Viking prince,' he laughed, and I assured him that my grandmother was a pure Swede.

'I've had many Turkish patients, Mr Harvard, but all of them ignorant of your world-class pianist İdil Biret. If you know who composed the piece we're listening to and who the pianist is, perhaps you can erase my negative impression of Turks.'

(Horowitz was my father's favourite pianist!) 'With your permission I'll reply to both questions. It's Chopin's Op. 55, Nocturne No. 2, and Vladimir Horowitz is playing.'

I recall his nervous laugh as he said, 'I must rush off to an important meal; bring your princess in right away.'

İz came in, head bent, timid as an inexperienced concubine, but when he put his hand on her shoulder and declared, 'I will give you your face back, Turkish Delight,' I felt like kissing his hands like they do in corny Turkish films.

İz could be operated on in four days. Ideally we should stay in London for five months afterwards. I was keenly aware that a long period of psychological adjustment would be inevitable. The doctor had warned us of the possibility.

The surgery, performed at the 'Let's Face It' clinic next to Chelsea's football arena, lasted three and a half hours. The Cypriot nurse, who embellished her Turkish with 'merci very' at every opportunity, would come with the 'good news'. During the clinical examination I rented a furnished flat in Park Lane. I was planning to go to Istanbul once a month for board meetings. My irrepressible uncle had gone on a 'live masturbation' tour of Egon Schiele's paintings in European galleries so I would have to supervise the daily business by telephone.

For the next four weeks İz went around with a gauze-like protective mask. She was sick from the continuous medication. She would tremble when the protective cream was being applied and sob with anger as she resisted the urge to scratch her face. I hit the streets after putting her to sleep, renewing my vow for revenge. Waiting by her dimly lit bedside to give her the necessary medication at two o'clock in the morning, I read through the complete works of Thomas Bernhard and Paul Auster.

The doctor was happy with his first examination, and he ended the mask application. Decreasing her doses he began the massage period which was to last for three months. When Gediz, İz's twin brother who thinks the Beatles killed pop music, came with their mother to visit, I went back to Istanbul for four days. The first night, after the board meetings, I met with the usual crowd at Hünkâr's for a meal. I knew that the ungrateful Güfte with her Byzantine tricks had taken over İz's job, and wouldn't turn up for the meal.

Superintendent Kasnak, whom I visited on the last day, thought I should abandon this girl, who would be overwhelmed by depression even if she did recover, and find a way to marry a European princess from the Ottoman dynasty. I knew I would find Cahid Hodja in the stockroom memorizing the dictionary on his makeshift table. I wasn't surprised he looked guilty and embarrassed when he saw me, but he was moved when I conveyed in great detail what had happened to us. I began my pre-prepared spiel with a prayer:

'… In the old days some joined religious sects to acquire "a visa for paradise" or "because of a herd mentality". They say that the unscrupulous Kutsi's father, a phony pilgrim, joined the sect to gain influence over trade, but he has won few contract tenders and has never worked in a public department. The hypocrite who uses all the loopholes in the financial system to pay less tax than a high-school teacher aspires to cultivate the state like his own farm through the contacts he has made with key people. While his mean-spirited son enjoys a life of pleasure and squanders the money they snatched out of people's mouths, my girlfriend, whom he almost killed, cries continuously with pain. The fact that this man is not sitting in some corner of a prison cell awaiting punishment, and the fact that the publishers to whom she gave her life ignore her situation out of fear, makes my blood boil, Cahid Hodja. If he doesn't serve his sentence my conscience will never rest! I'm ready to pay a fortune to anyone who will help me …'

I never expected him to cut me short like a Red Indian chief raising his hand.

'Do you hear what you're saying, Arda? What American university taught you to right one wrong with another? You're young and because your pain is fresh, your reaction is over the top. It is partly because well-brought-up young people like you don't get involved in politics and don't undertake public duties that the system remains underdeveloped. God forbid I would ever abuse my God-given gift and turn a weapon against any other servant of His. I wouldn't even shoot a goldfinch after what happened to me. While you rail against the injustice of the system you should not ignore the divine justice of Almighty God. There is no escape from His justice. And finally, how can you be sure that the fugitive Kutsi is not serving his divine sentence at this very moment?'

His reply, which was more terse than I expected, made me even angrier. 'You were the only one left who didn't talk in Gòd's name, Cahid Çiftçi,' I said. 'This country, supposedly in His name, has suffered enough from those who take advantage of the people's innocence. I will not rest in peace until Kutsi is buried in pain as deep as İz's. Besides, who can say that my attempt to punish him is not divine fate?'

I left without a farewell. We both knew that we probably wouldn't be seeing each other again.

I bought İz's favourite comics and offbeat magazines, chocolate-covered chestnuts and Sezen Aksu's two latest CDs before boarding the delayed plane.

İz's good spirits partially came back when her face healed faster than Dr Rohatgi had expected. Zuhâl and Zafer came for a surprise visit, and the second time I came back from a visit to Istanbul I brought back İfakat for a week. My uncle, on a vigorous masturbation tour of the pre-Christian nude sculptures in the Metropolitan Museum of Art, the Boston Museum and the Louvre, stayed with us while in London. From October İz started to socialize with ease. We had pleasant trips as far as Inverness with Nurse Serap and her computer expert husband. On my third trip to Istanbul I wrote a note to Kutsi Serhamza, immediately regretting it and beginning to fear my lack of self-confidence:

YOU WILL PAY YOUR PENALTY IN EXCESS!
YOURS PERMANENTLY
DEMON ...

İz's face had completely healed by mid-December. We chose to disregard the side-effects (partial loss of vision in her left eye and lack of movement of her eyebrows and forehead). On our last visit I invited Dr Rohatgi to Istanbul and gave him a silver cigarette-holder bearing the seal of Sultan Abdülhamit II. As he wished us goodbye he said, 'I know that you're wondering why I reject plastic surgery for my own ugly face. My dear Harvardite, it's because I dreamt that if a surgeon's hand touched my face I'd lose my gift.' I was reminded of Cahid Hodja's maxim that he would refuse to make use of his sharpshooting talent on any other human.

I wanted to embarrass Selçuk Altun as soon as I returned. I purchased a rare signed copy of a Graham Greene book, *A Gun for Sale*, from his favourite secondhand bookseller. (First I was going to whet his appetite by showing him the book, then I'd decide whether to give it to him or not.) Three days before our reunion with Istanbul, I took all the one and two pence coins collected in a kitchen jar to the slovenly girl who was breastfeeding her baby in Piccadilly Circus tube station.

'How many bottles of milk do you think I can get with these?' she chided.

It was clear from Zuhâl's tone of voice when she phoned in the early hours of the following morning that she had some shocking news.

'While I was wondering how to tell you one piece of news, I heard another I must tell you,' she said. 'The day before yesterday, while the treacherous shop owner and his family were picnicking in the Belgrade Forest, their shop and home above it were completely burned down. Yesterday evening when Kutsi was on his way to the Black Sea coast in his Mercedes, a lorry without a licence-plate smashed into him from the side and rolled him into a ditch. The poor bastard broke his neck and is now in a wheelchair! Arda, I thought such coincidences could only happen in films and novels ...'

In a panic, not knowing what to say, I called the shooting range. When I told Kasnak that I must speak to my Hodja, he said, 'You're going to have to commit suicide, my boy.' (Cahid Çiftçi had killed himself two weeks before.) Realizing we were returning to Istanbul at the weekend, he politely requested a bottle of Napoleon cognac.

Feeling as if I had been punched twice on the chin, I went to see İz packing her suitcase to the accompaniment of Sezen Aksu songs. I dramatically delivered Zuhâl's news. She bowed her head, perhaps to avoid seeing me lie, and asked, 'Were these things done under your orders, Arda?' (I realized her tone of voice was not accusing.) As I delicately caressed her face, fresher than a baby's, I'll never forget saying, 'If Cahid Hodja hadn't passed away two weeks ago, my answer might not have been "no".'

B

The prisoner is not the one who has committed a crime, but the one who clings to his crime and lives it over and over. We are all guilty of crime, the great crime of not living life to the full.

Sunday After the War by Henry Miller

Is it only an ugly fool who makes friends with mirrors? I consulted mine three times a day. When I heard what they said behind my back in Tarlabaşı – 'Can this ugly fellow be the son of such a handsome man as the actor Kadir İnanır?' – I thought I was suffering yet another of God's wrathful blows.

According to mankind's almanac, if a year of a dog's life is equivalent to 7½ years of a man's, doesn't that make me 300?

I reflected that if I had a twenty-year prison sentence for every life I'd taken, I'd lose count of what my total sentence should be.

Even without Gürsel Hodja's help I would have realised that books were treacherous friends. (But never let them spot your weakness.) I put aside forty of the least harmful and burned the rest as punishment.

I also realised that unless I confessed to the Hodja that I was a hit man, I would gradually be overcome by feelings of guilt. He refused to listen.

'I don't think you can tell me anything about yourself that I don't already know,' he said. 'The most mysterious part of the heaven or hell business is our lack of precise knowledge of the rules of entry. A naive murderer who has fallen into a trap goes to heaven; an honest bureaucrat who plunges his country into millions-of-dollars'-worth of damage can go to hell, because of an unintentional but serious mistake,' the holy man declared.

Did your faithful servant ever mention to you the final entry in a diary he kept?

The only good luck I ever had in my life was friendship with the wisest man in the city, who hid away among the permanently sick inhabitants of a hospital to escape from the chaos of the shallow life around him.

According to the Old Testament, blessed Noah's grandfather Methuselah lived for 969 years. And according to Isaac B. Singer, on the eve of the Flood he might have been feeling bored with life.

There's an excuse for murder, but no consolation for boredom ...

A

Is death male or female?

Ölüm (Death) by Muammer Gaddafi, 1996

When İz said she was moving in with me I thought she was joking. İfakat, hoping for some light and harmony in our home, accepted the situation as God's will.

I don't remember a more satisfying meal than the one we ate together on New Year's Eve, which consisted of gherkins, raw meatballs, take-away kebabs and Ottoman desserts. (Before retiring at midnight we watched a thought-provoking film which I chose at random from my father's collection.)[1] Two days later, İz began working as the public relations advisor at our firm. If my father had seen the striking essays she wrote in the provocative periodicals,

---

1   Sam Peckinpah's *Bring Me the Head of Alfredo Garcia.*

he would have said, 'Squirrel, kneel to your mother if you must, but don't let go of this marvellous girl.'

Despite the six zeros dropped from the Turkish lira, our companies were doing well and there were no comic messages from Uncle, who was busy exploring Californian landmarks which cropped up in William Saroyan's stories. Every morning I awoke feeling uneasy at my growing respect for İz. Suddenly I shivered at the words of the narrator of the book I was reading: 'My wife and children are in the next room. I am in good health and have enough money. Oh God, I'm most unhappy.'

(I must have been missing my guardian angel, appointed by my mother to protect me after her death.)

İz was glued to the television when she wasn't at work: cartoons and the Olympic Games in Athens. I saw she wanted to be left alone and was happy to slip down to the nearest cinema.

I was unexpectedly moved by a documentary film called *My Father, the Architect*, in which Nathaniel Kahn tries to discover his father Louis Kahn's face. It is a desert-like surface of craters caused by an accident he'd suffered as a baby in Estonia. When I suggested that İz might be interested in Kahn's character (he was ugly, warped and conceited) and in his disagreements with his contemporaries, all she said was, without moving her eyes from the television screen, 'I can't take an interest in anything more demanding than the trampoline finals.'

A second letter arrived at my office:

02.04.2005

My friend Arda Ergenekon,

Are you prepared to find out who murdered your father? You won't detest him more than I do.

As life is a three-act play, I propose to give you six clues in succession. (If you fluff your lines you don't get a second chance.)

If you reach the sixth stage, we'll destroy him together.

The first clue will be ready on 12.04.05; the second on 22.04.05.

Go with the prayer besmele[1] *to the Kariye Museum and find two numbers in the middle courtyard ...*

Apart from the late Cahid Hodja, the only people who knew I had begun to search for my father's killer were my simple-hearted uncle, the repulsive Selçuk Altun, İz and Adil Kasnak.

With a shudder I realized from the parentheses scattered randomly throughout his rapidly written novels that the letter, with its paranoid-like tone, belonged to Selçuk Altun. (It was time to tackle this psychopath; I didn't care if he thought me a halfwit and a lazy loafer.)

☙

[1] The Arabic formula *bismillah!*, meaning 'in the name of God the Compassionate, our Saviour', used particularly before starting a major project.

The Kariye Museum

I remembered journeys my father and I made to see the Valens Aqueduct and the chaotic wonders of the shop windows in Zeynel Abidin's music store. Then we would go on to Horhor where, according to my father, 'they stopped turning the pages of the calendar thirty years ago' and eat spiced meat pittas in a deserted pitta house.

I thought my father was joking when he said that during her *intrigues* a Byzantine empress had had an underground tunnel dug, three kilometres long, between the then royal Sultanahmet Mosque and Horhor. Passing along that route 1,000 years later, I felt as uneasy as though I was entering a foreign country. I imagined even Sultan Mehmet II, the conqueror of Istanbul, would have been startled to see such a parade of veiled pedestrians.

I thought the ugly buildings around the Kariye Museum, which has survived with its simple charm for 1,500 years, increased its appeal. The monument, which has been a church, then a mosque and most recently a museum, is known to charge foreign tourists three times the normal rate. At the entrance to the old-fashioned lavatory in the courtyard with its squat columns was a shoeblack's box, and inside Cappadocia souvenirs were being sold to the accompaniment of arabesque music. As though all the different kinds of glass in the windows overlooking the museum's dreary courtyard were not ugly enough, pages of tabloid newspaper were stuffed into broken panes. In the front section, ill-concealed by lofty trees, a disgusting plastic pipe of dirty water descended from roof to ground level. I was horrified – it was like throwing acid in the face of a beauty queen. I felt ashamed on behalf of dignified Kariye's nameless architects and its Byzantine and Ottoman guardians.

I knew the museum would not be busy on the eve of the season. The section of mosques and churches set aside for prayer is called *sahin* in Arabic. I wanted to look – perhaps for the last time – at the rare frescoes and mosaics in the old Kariye Church/Mosque. My father had said the thematic frescoes on the ceilings were 'Byzantium's most astounding visual works'. (He thought that Turkish artists after Nazmi Ziya had never begun to approach the profundity of the fresco called *The Assyrian Massacre*.) Tired of watching the hippy girl examining the frescoes in the outer narthex through her binoculars, and a chic Spanish couple quarrelling along from the tombs, I moved to the middle of the prayer-space. At the entrance to the observation area was a barricade of two-dozen female tourists, and I wasn't surprised when they yawned at the guide's silly spiel in bad English. I wondered wryly if I were a vulgar woman-hunter, which of these cellulite monuments would I choose?

I began to suspect that Selçuk Altun with his warped mind was going to offer clues that made fun of my father's passion for history and mathematics. I was summoned to the museum on 12 April to find two numbers, by a letter dated 2 April, in which words were fundamentally linked to numbers. I thought I might spot them as a pair or as two opposite points. When I eventually saw two giant icons in the wings of the motionless dome, I experienced the sheer relief of having completed an exam.

As the awe-inspiring numbers revolved in my head, I approached the magnificent mosaics full of hope.

When the site became a mosque in the sixteenth century, the eyes of the Blessed Jesus were made null and void. (But in the right wing, one can sense the dim foreknowledge in the concerned eyes of the Virgin Mary fixed on her baby.)

Along the base of the mosaics, which were two metres above the floor, hung protective covers two handspans long. I wasn't wrong in assuming that even a thief who was only partly alert would hide the clues under these covers, instead of right in the middle of the icons. I saw the numbers '38' and '248' carved with a knife at either end of the plastic protectors. Recalling the word *besmele* in the recent letter, I left the museum with the consolation that these two hastily carved numbers might convey some cruel textual message according to the alphanumerical cryptogram *Ebced*.[1]

I returned to the office in a taxi that said, 'Overtake at your own risk' on the boot. Until there was evidence, I knew I had to hide developments from İz, who wouldn't

---

1   A method of presenting a word or a phenomenon by assigning numbers to the Arabic alphabet.

allow the slightest criticism of Selçuk Altun. On the way I felt queasy at the idea of seeing eye-to-eye in the middle of a detective novel.

When I heard that Altun already possessed the book by Graham Greene which the author had signed with a dedication to his first mistress, Dorothy Glover, I decided to give the copy I brought from London to Professor Haluk Oral, a collector of signed books. With his help, I established that according to the basic *Ebced*, the fateful numbers '38' and '248' corresponded to 'the Executioners' Graveyard'.

○⃝

Cellatlar, the Executioners' Graveyard

Chasing after an insidious book he found in a secondhand bookshop, my uncle flew to Moscow to visit the eighty-one psychiatric hospitals of the Soviet Union period where intellectuals had been sent for 'treatment'. Meanwhile, in an article entitled 'Istanbul: City of the Good and Inconsiderate', İz wrote about how in a kebab house two people would struggle hopelessly to prevent the other picking up the bill, then the same two would destroy themselves in traffic, each refusing to give way. After Adil Kasnak, who became our Security Chief on 1 April, had read her article twice, he said, 'If your girlfriend were to write about the four billion loaves of bread dumped every year in the garbage in a country where 7,000,000 people survive on \$2 a day, would her readers disown her, my boy?'

I couldn't find anything on the Cellatlar, the Executioners' Graveyard in encyclopedias or on the internet. Before stress got the better of me, I rang Selçuk Altun. I knew he'd be helpful without giving much away. He directed me to the book-finder Nedret İşli, partner in a secondhand bookshop called Turkuaz. I warmed to Nedret and his colleague Puzant, who yelled at each other in the claustrophobic shop in a side street off Beyoğlu. (They weren't unhappy despite the considerable difficulties they faced running a secondhand bookshop in a country with a reading handicap.) According to the pamphlet[1] they had at hand, the graveyard was on a slope by the historic Pierre Loti Coffee House on the ridges of Eyüp Sultan district:

> Over the graves were erected thick stones of human height. Even though these executioners only fulfilled state orders, they have always been universally detested, buried separately, and never admitted into public cemeteries.

Hayrullah was supposed to be from neighbouring Karagümrük, but in spite of my warnings, he took two wrong turnings before he found the Pierre Loti Coffee House. The historic coffee house was renamed Pierre Loti,

---

1   *Eyüp Sultan Loti Coffee House and Surroundings* (1966), M. Mes'ud Koman.

after the eminent writer's frequent visits there to observe the panoramic view of Istanbul and the Golden Horn. My father thought that the Ottomans had shown exaggerated hospitality to Pierre Loti, that bizarre individual who led several lives, and he named the sincere enthusiasm for foreigners, whether Balkan folk-dancing groups or visiting football referees, 'the Pierre Loti syndrome'. In the coffee house, after coffee tasteless as İfakat's and reluctantly served by an overdressed waiter, conscious of the early spring silence, I walked uncertainly towards the Ottoman cemetery, consulting the 1/2,000-scaled map at the back of the pamphlet. On the rough terrain where the Executioners' Graveyard was said to be, there was a cemetery – perhaps a century old – of many gravestones that emphasized their Black Sea origins. The dark-skinned youth, who was walking with a spring in his step, seemed like a volunteer parking attendant and when I asked where the Executioners' Graveyard was, answered, 'By God, I don't know, I just came from the East a month ago.'

When two more people were alarmed by the word *Executioner* falling from my lips, I decided to call Altun once again. Withdrawing from the exploration site, I wandered around the neighbouring cemetery where the monumental gravestones of élite Ottomans stood, until I found the ruined tomb of Sultan Beyazid II's *şeyhülislam*,[1] who fathered 99 children. Walking in a still environment

---

1   (Formerly) the Grand Mufti, or head of the Islamic hierarchy responsible for all religious matters.

without walls to cut off the surroundings, I experienced a growing sense of inner ease and I turned back when I reached the eternal resting-place of Field Marshal Çakmak.

Hearing that I couldn't find what I expected on the Eyüp slopes, Altun of the nervous giggle pointed me in the direction of Eugenio Geniale, who invited me to drink *salep* with him the following night at his home in the Genoese district of Galata. I was impressed by the global list of inhabitants in the hallway of the monumental apartment block that was the size of a chateau. Ascending in the tired lift, I was startled to recall the seventy-something Geniale who, under the pseudonym Engin Genal, had written books on architecture and was a walking encyclopedia who spewed out his knowledge at any opportunity. Just as I went to touch the bell, the door opened halfway with a rhythmic creak. I thought the blue-eyed giant with the reddish-grey beard resembled both Santa Claus and the Ottoman admiral Barbaros. Noticing I was looking at his purple apron, the Levantine art historian declared, 'I was baking you an apple tart' and as soon as he heard my name he began to announce at the door, 'Arda actually means flowing water, it's our only river that hasn't changed its name since the early ages. The word used for flowing water or a spring in Armenian is *aru* and in old Farsi it's *adea* …' I inwardly cursed the sadistic Selçuk Altun until his greeting was over. As I toured the spacious high-ceilinged flat, which even had a toilet with a view of Topkapı Palace,

I stepped hesitantly on the silk carpets. On the walls of the living room hung plaques of Ottoman calligraphy with seals; and there were orientalist nude paintings in the bedroom. I thought the engravings by the utopian architect G. B. Piranesi perfectly suited the mahogany bookcases in his study. To my question, 'Were you fond of Louis I. Kahn?', he replied, 'He used to sit in front of a Piranesi engraving in his chaotic office in Philadelphia.'

The attractive young woman whom he scolded in Russian, and who brought tart and coffee to the antique armchair in the drawing room where I was timidly ensconced, was clearly not his maidservant. Instead of coming to the main point of the evening and departing, I felt like making this ancient Levantine talk. I knew that indicating the family photo on the central table was enough to start off his autobiographical harangue: 'I am the last member of a Genoese family that has lived in Galata since the fourteenth century and has never broken ties with Istanbul. Thanks to our ancestors, who grew wealthy by trading in textiles during Byzantine and Ottoman times, for the last 200 years no Geniale has had to work. I know the Byzantine and Ottoman monuments stone by stone. I recognize them from their moans with my eyes shut. I have visited every harbour city on this planet that has a museum. I spent so much time reading and learning languages that I had no time to write anything of my own. To decipher manuscripts in dying languages is a great passion of mine. If I go before him I will leave my 2,000 manuscript treasures to Selçuk Altun. The moment I lose my immunity to the beast that harasses the body and soul of Istanbul, I will flee to my sister in Genoa.'

I was touched by the grateful glow in his eye when he told anecdotes about his parents. (It is interesting how Levantines are not orientalized when it comes to a question of family.) As Anna, his companion, dashed from the living room after a reprimand for serving cognac in the wrong glasses, I announced my reason for being there: 'Sir, I am preparing a piece for a competition for amateur novelists. My narrator is searching for his father's killer, and has to find a succession of clues in six historic places. I don't know why, but the second location I selected was the Executioners' Graveyard. I'm sorry to say I couldn't find it on the Eyüp slopes. Instead of giving up I thought that discovering the reason might help the flow of my work ...'

'One shouldn't be surprised at people who lack respect for the dead when they are incapable of embracing the *living*. We have become a people with a limited sense of history, enjoying the occasional successes on the battlefield and the silly tales of womanizing pashas. Even though the recruited executioners remained outcasts even in their burial, the fact that a cemetery was allocated at holy Eyüp is quite meaningful. During the uncontrolled expansion of the city the place became a public cemetery. The insensitive people who have allowed the earth of the newly dead to be thrown on top of the old graveyard have damaged the historic fabric of Eyüp for ever.

'Gigantic rectangular stones, roughly carved, used to be erected as headstones for the executioners. When the subject crops up again once every forty years I remember what a startling sight these dark, pitted and nameless stones presented as a group. The only help I can give you is to try and find a photograph in my archives that hasn't yet seen the light of day,' he said.

As soon as I looked at the faded photo in a Venetian cardboard box that Anna brought him I realized at once how I could arrive at the clue, and I could hardly refrain from shouting with joy. Handing back the photo while trying to conceal my excitement, I longed impatiently for morning.

On my way out I couldn't resist asking how he and Selçuk Altun had met.

'He came just like you to ask for help with the novel he was writing,' he said, but when he added, 'He really *did* write one', I was embarrassed by a sudden, fleeting reproachful look in his blue eyes.

On the way down in the lift, I reproached myself for not immediately realizing his involvement in Selçuk Altun's plot.

For the last time I went to the old Executioners' Graveyard, consoled by the fact that İz wouldn't press me even if she knew I was up to something. On my first visit I had noticed on my way down the hill the difference in one of the steps. I had observed in the photograph Geniale showed me that this particular step had been converted

from one of the special headstones used in the Executioners'
Graveyard. Very respectfully I approached the old porous
stone that looked as if a squad of executioners had fired
hundreds of bullets at it and reflected that the aesthetic
Geniale would foam at the mouth with rage if he saw the
last monumental element of a historic site being used as a
stepping stone. On two sides of a little piece of cardboard
I pulled out from the largest crevice in the stone, 'İZNİK'
and 'NİCE' were written in pen.

In primary school I had learned from my father that
the city names of İznik and Nice were borrowed from
Nike, the Goddess of Victory. In Istanbul, when you say
'Nike', the first monument that comes to mind is my
father's favourite – the fifth-century Kıztaşı (the Maiden
Stone) in the Fatih district. I withdrew, happy to be near
the Maiden Stone on the morning of 2 May.

Altun must have decided to give his plaything a double
clue in case I took off for İznik. Was he amusing himself
by treating me like a reasonably intelligent person in the
first two rounds, but trying to raise the tension in the
next? That night, awoken by a massive cramp in my left
calf from a dream in which I learned that Altun was my
father, I began to wonder about the extent of my mother's
relationship with this strange family friend.

ᎧᏂ

Kıztaşı, the Maiden Stone

By the time of the Harkov lap of his psychiatric safari in the Ukraine, my uncle was physically exhausted but came racing back home. In her article 'A Mirror of the Person Who Cannot Use Paper Money', İz's starting point was the inhuman way in which our paper money gets worn away and disintegrates, and suggested that our public toilets were dirtier than those in African countries. I'm wary of İz dishing up other articles in the same tone as my father's reactionary writings.

During İz's painful convalescence in London I used to take refuge in the bottomless pit of the city's metro system to avoid seeing the healthy, lively, giggling faces of the young girls who flood the streets. (Even a part-time idler doesn't tire of the gloomy world of the metro. I find the songs of the illegal buskers that echo through its corridors therapeutic. The boredom of crowds of weary citizens waiting at the mouth of the tunnel becomes a tourist's delight in a lunapark safari.) Apart from a certain apprehension that I might see Dalga coming up the escalator as I went down, I enjoyed the shelter of the underground. At the finish of the Athens Olympic Games, İz was concentrating on the US Open. I didn't tell her – she might have taken it amiss – that she reminded me of the Swiss tennis-player Patty Schnyder. During the final of the women's pole-vaulting, she said, 'Come and see what a pretty girl looks like.' But I was pleased when she failed to get very excited by the record-breaking Yelene Isinbayeva, who was just like a young Dalga.

The granite column erected for the Emperor Markianos by Tatianus, the governor of Constantinople in the fifth century, was known as 'Kıztaşı' (the Maiden Stone) after the sculptures of the Goddess of Victory (Nike) on the north panel of the pedestal. When the surroundings were cleared by a neighbourhood fire of 1908, a column seventeen metres high could no longer lie hidden in a private garden. The elegant grey stone column, formed of a single piece, had the look of an orphan just emerging from a fire. Whenever we visited the Maiden Stone after a feast in a pitta house in Horhor, my father would remember the note by M.S.,[1] who crammed the *Complete Illustrated Ottoman Encyclopedia* into 350 pages, and he would laugh in annoyance.

The Maiden Stone gives its name to a quiet street in a dignified district and when I came across it for the first time after his death, I felt like a ship at sea sighting a friendly lighthouse. I had never noticed the care taken that the buildings around it should not exceed its height. It was as though the quiet locality that lived in a different era was silent out of respect and solicitude. The Byzantine monuments seemed to have hypnotized the neighbouring buildings and city-dwellers. A polite passer-by idling along

---

[1]   On it was a statue of the Emperor Markianos (451–457). There was a rumour that it could tell if girls who walked past were virgins or not. It was even reported that the statue broke when Justinian II played the same trick on his sister-in-law.

even showed a concealed parking-spot in a side street to Hayrullah, who thought the Maiden Stone was a structure erected on the Independence Day celebrations at the time of Atatürk, and had then been forgotten. As I approached the column I felt it had shrunk. While not surprised that disgusting weeds had embraced the pillar, concealing it till it became a rubbish dump for plastic bottles, I couldn't come to terms with the abandonment of a stone column, thus depriving history of an inscription that summarized 1,500 years of its past. At a time of column vandalism, I hated to see a campaigning poster for local government elections hanging at a height that only a giraffe could reach.

Like an amateur seer I approached the statue of Victory with apprehension. Seeing nothing bigger, I gently inserted my hand into a crack. When I thankfully withdrew it there were three centimetres of a small yellow pencil between my index and forefingers. I saw a few short words in Arabic, Latin, Greek and Armenian etched with a needle-point on four faces of the hexagonal clue.

To reward myself with a bottle of spring water at the end of the third round, I approached a little kiosk, but when I saw its tragi-comic poster I nervously withdrew.

It worried me that the name 'Titanic' on the shop door was either a joke or the product of a skewed mentality. I felt my neck prickle at an imaginary pair of eyes. If they didn't actually belong to my guardian angel he would send them back where they belonged.

According to the owners of the Turkuaz bookshop, who thought I was writing fiction, my fourth clue was 'The Oldest Sacred Building'. When I rang Eugenio Geniale he said, 'If you're not writing your autobiography you're up to something very dodgy,' and I thought he was going to hang up on me. The Holy Church of St John the Baptist, which was the oldest sacred building in the city, built in the fifth century, had been open for worship for 1,000 years and was re-baptized as the İmrahor Mosque. Now I could wait calmly and with pleasure for 12 May, satisfied that Selçuk Altun would be just a little more perplexed after every round.

ॐ

The İmrahor Mosque

I was quite expecting some new eccentricity from my uncle when he invited me to dinner at the Pidos Pizzeria. In the reams of paper he brought along there were forty thought-provoking street names chosen from 48,000 locations in the index of the *Istanbul Atlas*. While we were drinking coffees on-the-house he was dreaming of the socio-cultural safaris he would follow from the names he put in a bag from which İz would choose twenty. To avoid upsetting the quiet mystery of these streets, he would take arty photographs of them. To struggle free from her own quagmire, İz would turn her days in the media merry-go-round of business and politics into a cartoon novel headed

The Final Downfall of the Naive Mystic. The chief managers of the Sultan's stables were called *İmrahor.* On the eve of the *İmrahor* project I met a dopey banker for a business lunch at the Four Seasons and was delighted to see in a strategic corner of the restaurant, my father's friend Judith the pianist and her bibliophile husband Tunç Uluğ. I rose to greet them, sure the elegant couple wouldn't ask me when I intended to get married, but noticing they were sharing a table with Selçuk Altun and his wife, I beat a hasty retreat. He might have been calculating whether he had crammed his fourth clue into the easiest hole as he was eating his risotto. On the way to Çamlıca I couldn't bear the idea that he might use İz and Adil Kasnak as a tool and a hitman.

Somehow my father had never been able to include Samatya in his world, the one district, he said, whose name had never changed since the founding of Byzantium. I noticed that even cars driving along the depressing streets took care not to blow their horns. Apart from a few religious buildings scattered at intervals on both sides of the road, there was the pleasing sight of an abandoned Greek kiosk and an Ottoman mansion with a balcony. I couldn't help stopping to eat *tulumba*, the cake soaked in syrup, in the Rumeli cakeshop and asked the whereabouts of the İmrahor Mosque. On an election poster by the road alongside the mosque which trailed along like a superannuated museum on its last legs, I wasn't surprised to see, as well as an Armenian young man, a committee of elderly mustachioed candidates. The high-walled building opposite, which resembled a medieval tower, was converted to a mosque in 1486 by a sultan's charismatic master of the royal stables.

The swarthy youngster saw me waiting passively at the gate of the building whose registration number was 193891, and swaggered over to tell me that the museum was officially closed and I could visit only by permission from some head office. I wasn't deterred. Believing my tolerant companion wouldn't mind, I took a good look at the enormous fig tree that spread across the courtyard and at the other huge trees whose names I didn't know. Beginning at the south wing I followed the henna-coloured bricks of a powerful wall, and saw with pleasure the west wing embellished with the names of heroes from the eastern provinces, opposite a park with red-tiled paths that matched the colour of the secluded museum. Groups of women were seated at separate tables, veiled or in low-cut dresses as though it was spring. A bunch of pensioners dozed in the shade or stared vacantly around like finalists in a competition for the most tragi-comic face. I recalled sad photographs in the *Istanbul Encyclopedia from Yesterday to Today* of the remains of the obscure museum on the verge of turning into a rubbish dump. Like an unfinished Kahn project, the museum with its geometrical floor design as enchanting as a silk carpet was a remarkable monument. It had survived the 1782 fire and the earthquake of 1894, but in 1908 the roof had collapsed under heavy snow and now it would never be repaired. I walked through the main gate feeling uneasily that I was a citizen of a country that didn't even have the sensitivity of an Ottoman stable master.

I pushed my old comb into an inviting crack parallel to the identification plate of the edifice and a piece of cardboard, the size of a matchbox, fell to the ground. As the afternoon ezan began, I picked up a fateful yellow document which consisted of the words 'HADIM'[1] and 'ATİK'.[2]

I tried to figure out this fresh clue in the light of the first three. 'Hadım' and/or 'Atik' might be the nickname of a pasha who had a monument built to the Ottoman dynasty in his own name. According to the information in two different encyclopedias, Hadım Ali Paşa, head of a religious foundation, was twice appointed Grand Vizier in the time of Sultan Beyazid II, and in contemporary sources was referred to as Atik Ali Paşa. (My father would have said, 'There can't be a more suitable word than *atik* to describe someone who can rise from pimping to becoming prime minister.') The fifth clue must be the mosque at Çemberlitaş in the Atik Ali Paşa complex of buildings named after its philanthropic donor who converted the Kariye Church to a mosque.

CR

---

1   Eunuch.
2   Energetic.

The Atik Ali Paşa Mosque

My uncle's mission was brought to an abrupt end when the locals on the various streets objected to him photographing their children without permission. On the eve of my expedition to Çemberlitaş, he flew to Stockholm to attend the funeral of his only cousin. While travelling he heard news that his contemporary, Bjorn, who had encouraged him on his series of controversial journeys, had died of a heart attack.

'I feel death prowling round me on every side,' he commented.

After his last duty to his favourite cousin, he would set out on a safari to the ten most outrageous striptease clubs in Europe, the playground of male beauties. İz, meanwhile, had postponed her comic novel project when she was offered a job as journalist-editor for a weekly magazine. In her first article for them, which she wrote under the pseudonym Baltazar Satırbaşı, she satirized those mediocre writers who considered themselves great authors when their superficial books became bestsellers.

I was trying to decipher the book of miscellaneous collages called *Suicide Bridge* by Iain Sinclair. I had bought the book because of these lines:

I understand now your passion to face the West. It is the passion for the extinction of yourself and the knowledge of the triumph of your own will in your body's extinction. But in the great periods, when man was great, he faced East.

As I walked past the Constantine Column, a casualty of restoration, erected in the fourth century by the Emperor Constantine, I deeply lamented Kıztaşı, the Maiden Stone. Surrounded by walls, the mosque's cemetery consisted of a plain tomb and artistic worn-out gravestones covered with wire mesh. I had seen similar precautions taken in zoos to protect the wild animals from human harassment. As soon as I passed through the main gate with a silent prayer, I seemed to have slipped down a time tunnel into the sixteenth century. I felt at ease in the calm and harmonious environment, half-closing my eyes in the midst of the five domes of the Atik Ali Paşa Mosque and all that belonged to it. The way people were wrapped in immediate silence as they entered the three gates into the spacious courtyard was impressive. I couldn't help hearing the inviting sound of the fountain opposite the mosque entrance. I walked respectfully across the courtyard to the fountain and saw the notice above, 'Please Do Not Take Large Canfuls of Water.' (But my stomach turned when I saw the label stuck where it was most visible, 'Pest Extermination Service'.) Reading the sign over the workshop door by the fountain, 'Apprentice Diamond-setter Wanted', I wondered what qualifications were required and how the surrounding studios of silver-workers could operate without making a sound.

As I viewed the mosque's façade of cut sandstone, I noticed four attached buildings to the left of the courtyard. It was interesting to see cobblers and grocery-stores creating income for the mosque complex under the old buildings rented out to silver wholesalers. Were the construction date and the architect of this geometrically simple and architecturally attractive monument deliberately kept unclear? A notice was stuck to the giant cylindrical columns in front of the main gate, 'Please Do Not Touch The Columns.' I remained poking my head through the door of the monumental building. Feeling subconsciously guilty because I knew only one basic prayer, I was startled too by an atmosphere of sublimity that was 500 years old. As one who doesn't evade his property tax and is incapable of planning anything wicked, I wondered why I should feel such a spiritual pressure. 'I doubt the therapeutic value of praying five times a day,' my sceptical father used to grumble.

I moved to a mound of earth as big as a child's grave in the centre of the courtyard. With my index finger I pulled out a tiny roll of paper from a tube connected to a sapling as thick as my thumb. On it was written:

The Lecturer and Judge
Gave His Own Name to the Fountain He Built
To Give Joy to the Soul of His Daughter
Who Died Eighteen Years Before Him.

I bought two books on Istanbul's public fountains. *Su Güzeli* (Water Beauty), illustrated with colour photographs, was published by the Municipality of Istanbul. I was sure that reading through the life-stories of 143 public fountains and discovering the last rendezvous would give me emotional indigestion. Instead of struggling with too many clues, some of them insoluble, I had to come to terms with these journeys. A few steps down any street could reveal different worlds; a journey of ten minutes could go back 1,000 years. I was finding serenity in these unique worlds, reluctant to share my dreams with my real life. If the last clue could find my father's vulgar psychopath killer, I knew I must deliver him to the police by means of Adil Kasnak. But the real problem was to trap paranoid Selçuk Altun, who was enjoying directing the whole drama from behind the scenes. My only chance to checkmate this repulsive chess-player who was moving me back and forth through the city was to find an unexpected weak point in his last clue. I was eager to see İz's face when I caught him redhanded, and figured out his rôle in the plot and just how much it was to his advantage. I knew that if I failed, that secretive man would abuse me in one of his hastily scribbled novels (if my mother were in my place, wouldn't she first convince my father's killer to get rid of Altun, then have the killer gunned down by her new hitman?).

I concentrated on the nostalgic photographs of *Su Güzeli*, knowing every page would make me sad. I could almost see how these ruined fountains, neglected treasures, would illuminate their surroundings once their façades were restored. I began to absorb these miniature monuments with the grand names, paragraph by paragraph, to the music of Pat Metheny. By the time I reached the Merzifonlu Kara Mustafa Paşa Fountain, I had digested the whole book.

It dawned on me that I would find the fatal clue at the end of the book in the section on the fountains in Üsküdar. The only Water Beauty engraved by the important orientalist artists, Eugene Flandin and W.H. Bartlett, was the Sadeddin Efendi Fountain, and I looked longingly at the engravings, but sadly at the warning lesson of the tragi-comic photographs. The identifying entry in the book reads as follows:

It lies on the right side of the street that leads to Tunusbağı, following the angle of the Karacaahmet tomb. It was built in 1741 (AH 1154) by Sadeddin Efendi, son of Kazasker Feyzullah Efendi, and grandson of Şeyhülislam Hodja Sadeddin Efendi – who wrote Tacü' t-Tevarih (The Domain of Islam) – to bless the soul of his dying daughter Zübeyde. Sadeddin Efendi was a lecturer; during his post as a mullah in Egypt he acted as judge in Mecca and Istanbul and died in 1759. He lies in an open tomb behind the fountain ...

I knew my eternal headache would come back when I read it for the second time. I wondered what kind of hateful plan that treacherous man from Üsküdar had in mind when he chose a location for the clue which was almost next to my parents' graves. I felt my hair stand on end. I hurled the laptop at the television screen in my office. My faithful secretary rushed in right away, and for the first time in my life I scolded her and threw her out. Probably it was good for me to notice I was becoming like my mother. I immediately took two aspirins. As therapy I started to count the moon-faced village children in the Oya Katoğlu painting right before me. My mother had continued to collect Elias Canetti's books of aphorisms even after my chatterbox father's death. In his last book I recalled him saying, 'From pain felt at the root there is no escape, it is understood, endured and preserved, it creates a poet.' And as I began to encourage myself, 'Come on Arda!', I warmed to my theme and continued, 'Show them, old chap, what pain can do when it's fuelled by hatred, curiosity and boredom.'

∝

The Fountain of Sadeddin Efendi

June – the month I could never adapt to, although I utter its name with pleasure. When his safari of eroticism ended, my uncle, with his new friend, disabled Gun, would head for the foothills of the Himalyas to look for snow leopards.

'I've already begun to tremble with excitement at the

thought of coming eye-to-eye with the majestic cats who wrap their body-long tails around themselves to fend off the cold. I'm sure, Arda, this mystical journey is going to be a turning-point in my life,' he had said.

During her morning walks in her comical tracksuit on the slopes of Çamlıca, İz made friends with more people in twenty-eight days than I had done in twenty-eight years. She was putting together an article, 'The Ten Most Important Living Poets According to Poet Güven Turan'.[1] I began reading Gerhard Köpf's dilemma-ridden novel, *There Is No Borges.*

Before my walk along Nuhkuyu Street to the Karacaahmet Cemetery I entered the beans-and-rice canteen where I knew I would be greeted by photographic landscapes of the eastern Black Sea.

I took care not to miss the attractive names of the side streets as I walked smartly between the buildings like a foreman. The insurance brokerage office, the test-tube baby unit, the hospital and the Üsküdar Courts of Justice building were lined up diagonally opposite me as though by divine providence. Random groups – kebab house, kiosk, hair salon, mobile phone outlet, coffee house – had invaded the street. The fountains of nicotine coffee houses ran the most lucrative businesses. Another element of chaos was the legion of over-elaborate name-plates for hundreds of

[1]   Adonis / İlhan Berk / Yves Bonnefoy / Eugenio de Andrade / Louise Glück / Geoffrey Hill / Philippe Jacottet / Mario Luzi / W.S. Mervin / Wislawa Szymborska.

small businesses. As I drew closer to Karacaahmet, marble workshops that looked like warehouses began to appear beneath the buildings where faded curtains were rarely opened. A gravestone supplier upstairs and a solicitor's office downstairs were as comic in their incongruity as a caricature. The moustachioed salesman who saw me looking closely at the cruel shop display of gravestones for children and young adults invited me in to show me the rest of the range …

As the endless walls of Karacaahmet began, the Felliniesque plateau of Nuhkuyusu disappeared. I realized, as soon as I turned into Tunusbağı Street, that since my mother died I hadn't been to visit my parents' graves.

The fountain, situated on the axis of the mosque, graveyard and tomb, and now being used for ablutions, resembled a silent popular hero who had lost his appeal in exile. I had to chuckle when I saw the sentence, in the 1938 publication on *Istanbul Fountains*, 'Its architecture shows the influence of Turkish *rococo*.' Around the Sadeddin Efendi tomb were graves with artistic tombstones. I was looking at the mosque graveyard through the makeshift railings above the wall, when I noticed the displaced stones abandoned by a rubbish-heap.

The inscription on the dry fountain, behind which I put my hand praying for the last clue, was as follows:

This World is a Dinner-table
Desires Come and Go

If you Have Found Us
Don't Wish for Anything Else
To Drink
1970

My right hand checked the tired stone notch by notch and found it empty, but I didn't panic and didn't think of searching for the last clue elsewhere. Perhaps my puppeteer had been held up and couldn't make his appointment in time, or perhaps he was testing my determination by directing me to meeting places with the most obvious features. Next day I set out with enthusiasm, but making no progress began to feel a bit uneasy. On the third, I tried some channels unheard-of even in detective novels; I even tried without success to decipher the message on the inscription, written in hopeless Turkish. Then I took stock of the situation in the shadow of the neighbouring bins where the street garbage was dumped. If I returned empty-handed from my 5 June outing, I would have to start thinking of virtual clues.

෪

A wedding procession of old-fashioned motor vehicles poured from İnadiye Camii Street as I walked on, determined to say goodbye to my fountain. (I'm quite fond of my personal prejudice that girls who have weddings accompanied by motorcades end up with unhappy homes.) As if taken over by a hidden force, I plunged into the street bordered by the cemetery where carpets were hung on the wall to dry. I noticed an old but still working toilet. I tried to enjoy the message on the name-plate:

> Sultan N. Mehmed's
> Head cook Pervane
> Mehmed Efendi was built AH 1055.
> 1641 M.
> In 1935 it was
> Abandoned and in 1993
> Was Rebuilt.

I walked very slowly towards the heart of the street. I thought the old men and women who leaned out of the windows of the wooden buildings to see the wedding procession had taken up poses worthy of a ceremonial photo. Enviously I watched the ever-happy children playing alongside those Ottoman buildings beside the dimly lit grocery store, the deserted bakery and the tiny cobblers' shops that were impervious to earthquakes, floods and ignorance. I realized I wasn't upset by my proximity to my mother's grave, she who had robbed me of my childhood happiness in return for unimaginable wealth.

I continued my walk down Bakırcılar Yokuşu Street. Ready to criticize people who dropped plastic bags near the cemetery, I noticed the surprising sign that permitted rubbish on the street only twice a week. The last frame that stuck in my mind from the peaceful street was of a preoccupied lady, blowing her cigarette smoke at the neighbouring cemetery from the second-floor window of a ramshackle building. She reminded me of the actress Jessica Lange.

Under a postmodern bower near the Fountain for Mihrimah Valide Sultan was a group of happy retired people. Assuming they had an average age of seventy-five, I wondered what they had left to laugh about.

I'd never have thought there could be such congestion on a Sunday in the triangle of mosque, tomb and cemetery. With shabby cars blocking the fountains, the turquoise inscription over the grilled window became more apparent. The sunny-faced caretaker who looked after the area for ablutions squinted at me, trying to remember where he'd seen me before. I thought the ancient man had dedicated himself to tending the forgotten fountain for nothing until I saw the signs, 'Pay the Fee for the Toilet' and 'Turn off the Taps'. I knew that if for the last time I stuck my hand behind the mute inscription, I would pull it back empty. I stood up satisfied I had done what I could. My eyes darkened and I seemed to enjoy it.

I set off from the Karacaahmet wing, not knowing where I would stop. If my puppeteer's intention was to make me acknowledge the overlooked Byzantine and Ottoman monuments and their adjacent worlds which clung so closely to life, at least he had succeeded. But suddenly I was annoyed with myself for my exaggerated view of him. I recalled the timeless journeys I had taken with my father. I would look at him with admiration and wait for the signal to head towards a kebab or pitta house.

When the noon ezan started, I bowed my head while examining the plots of land in the cemetery alongside the street, and wondered if they were deliberately set aside for those who died young. If my devil started to put pressure on me again – 'Your father is a Balkan Georgian, your mother a Jewish–Swedish mix. Your environment has no notion of the colour of your hair and eyes, and when you have money you can't even remember the amount, so what are you doing, lingering in this land of shadows?'– then I prayed the notes from the ezan would come to my rescue.

I walked as far as Mabeyin, to its outskirts with streams of water trickling over rocks. Eating raw meatballs in the courtyard of a kebab house converted from an Ottoman mansion in the shade of vast pine trees, I came to the conclusion that leaving no clue at the Sadeddin Efendi Fountain was a deliberate move, and that in order to track down my father's killer I had to sort and arrange *at length* what was in hand. With a male voice bellowing, 'Don't you worry …' on the primitive cassette-player in the shoddy taxi I entered, I thought uneasily, 'Am I the victim of an organized joke, or am I living through a bad dream?'

જી

I was eager to shut myself up in my study. Before surrendering gratefully to Pat Metheny, I searched for a common characteristic among the six meeting points:

Kariye and İmrahor were converted from churches to mosques / A layer of earth was dumped on top of the Executioners' Graveyard / One of the two Nikes of Kıztaşı had gone astray / Hadım Ali became Atik Ali Paşa Mosque / and The fountain in the Karacaahmet complex (Karacaahmet who rose from being a sultan's son to become a dervish) was intended for his deceased daughter but destined for her father, the judge.

Keeping the 'duality' of each one in mind and knowing they wouldn't produce an acronym, I put my clues in the order they were presented to me:

1. The Kariye Museum
2. Cellatlar, the Executioners' Graveyard
3. Kıztaşı, the Maiden Stone
4. The İmrahor Mosque
5. The Atik Ali Paşa Mosque
6. The Karacaahmet Cemetery (the Sadeddin Efendi Fountain)

I noticed that three of them started with the letter 'k'. Writing down in order the ones that didn't start with 'k' and concentrating on the capitals, I seemed to be trying to bide my time. 'C', 'İ', 'A', I thought. I hoped to God it wasn't 'CAHID' with two letters missing. With an inward prayer I grabbed an Ottoman–Turkish dictionary. Could this be my father's killer? This idler whose surname 'Çiftçi', signifying both 'a Jekyll-and-Hyde character' and 'farmer', emphasized his ambiguous qualities of diligence and denial? My hair stood on end when I thought that this repressed man, who hides behind a false name which oscillated between password and confession, spoke like a philosopher but when necessary could also wield a gun like a maestro.

Didn't he look more like a precise and mysterious serial killer than a psychopathic triggerman? When he sneaked back and amused himself at the expense of the police who couldn't catch him, I had to admit fate had brought us together. My father would say, 'The scientist who cannot analyse the concept of fate can never question the existence of God.'

I knew I could corner Adil Kasnak in a snug eating place where they cooked sheep's chitterlings on a spit. Requesting him politely not to burp into his phone, I asked him if he had been at Cahid Hodja's funeral. I wasn't surprised when he said he had heard the news of his suicide by phone, from a grocery store owner who claimed to be a relation. I couldn't believe that I'd shared my distress with my father's killer, whose apathetic attitude had tricked me into confiding in him. I was apprehensive that this man might do me harm. He had seen my deep distress at the time of İz's accident, and left the guilty runaway crippled, then went on to burn down the house and shop of his accomplice. I wanted to meet this twin-souled killer who had rescued my honour and probably my life by shooting the aggressor Seydo, even though he had said, 'I will not use my God-given talent for using a gun on any of His servants.'

Assuming my father's killer and my saviour really wanted to meet me, and hoping to find a final clue at the shooting range, I knew I could find the tramp Kasnak at a card table.

Out of respect for his concentration, I whispered, 'If you don't ask the reason why, and if you find anything of Cahid Hodja's left at the shooting range, two bottles of the best cognac for you.'

∾

When I first saw the name Bedirhan Öztürk on the second page of the Ottoman–Turkish dictionary brought by the swaggering Kasnak, I was startled by the way the names Arda, Bedirhan and Cahid were insinuated *alphabetically* into it. On page 22 appeared the street name that Bedirhan Cahid called Eşrefsaat, describing it as 'with God's permission, my dwelling and my grave'. I realized that when I entered the poetry competition Eşrefsaat was the street in Üsküdar which I'd chosen as an address from the directory – not knowing that was where my father had been shot.

Failing to see an additional hint on page 222, I felt that the virtual noose around me was tightening for the very last time.

∾

On the evening of 12 June, when İz went off for a four-day trip to Cappadocia with her girlfriends, I took a taxi to Eşrefsaat Street. I intended to check out the location of Bedirhan Cahid's lair then go straight home. Since he had concealed the number of his door, he must have thought I could spot it by some particular feature that would identify him. (Wouldn't it be better if he noticed I couldn't finish the last round? Even if he yelled that he was ready with a written confession I was far from sure that I wanted him to be punished.)

I imagined the meeting between my father and his killer with two souls. To escape this image, I focused on the neighbouring two-storey wooden building painted red. From the ground floor of this dark building, a dim light emitted a sudden spark that branded my brain and soul. A huge black handkerchief was held over my face: once again I was embarking on a journey through a dark tunnel as in a hypnotic trance, yet I had no fear though I had lost my mother and my guardian angel.

When I came round I knew I was a prisoner in that mysterious house. Struggling to see the time in the light by the bed where I'd lain, I realized my hands were handcuffed. (For a moment I felt proud to be so important.) I must have been out for forty minutes or so. I could hear Bedirhan Cahid upbraiding a young man called Asım in the next room, with the terrifying bark of a brutal army sergeant. Dismissing his assistant with a voice like a firecracker, he began to walk firmly towards the claustrophobic room. I regretted I hadn't closed my eyes before he put on the light. I knew at once he wouldn't speak and I wasn't surprised when I saw he wasn't lame. In the spacious drawing room into which he dragged me the furnishings were packed randomly as though at the last minute. I wondered at the empty shelves and the absence of books. In the huge photograph that had not yet been removed from the wall I had to look twice at the angry man in the Berkeley t-shirt. Was the hit man secretly smiling at my close interest in the portrait of a man who resembled my father? My attention was drawn to two green velvet armchairs face to face in the middle of the room. Without removing my handcuffs he sat me down on the chair with a view of the sea and squatted in front of me, a plastic bag in his hand.

'I'll try and come to the point, and please God, I won't bore you. Don't worry if you don't get a chance to speak, a more important duty is in store for you.

'A poor, lonely outsider, I'd just come back from army service and cleaned up a gang of thugs who had robbed and raped my 80-year-old adopted grandmother. My first duty as a hired killer was to obey your mother's orders to punish your paedophile father. When the pervert (whom you know) gave me the job, to whet my appetite he claimed your late father was a snobbish, arrogant enemy of religion who lived off his wife's money. For twelve years I put up with being used as a killing-machine in similar scenarios. I had no doubt that my future victims, even though they were supposed to be enemies of religion, were also at the very least sex-maniacs, blackmailers or tax-evaders.

'How much my satisfaction in hunting human prey increased by making you run from one clue to another! I was being paid good money to punish these sinners and had no need to put up with anyone else's whims.

'I slept peacefully in my cocoon spun from books and beliefs. If I hadn't gotten to know the philosopher hiding inside the eccentric garment you see in that picture on the wall, I could have gone on rotting away.

'When my employer noticed I was waking up I eliminated him before he could lay a hand on me. Unless I swore to take no more lives from then on I wasn't ever going to free myself from my inner distress. As a cheap serial killer I certainly deserved to be punished. I was drowning in a whirlpool of despair deeper than the pangs of conscience.

'I was disgusted by a system which used religion principally as a means to political and financial ends, was insensitive to history and tradition, and was subject to recurrent socio-economic failures. As my anger with the books responsible for my loneliness gradually increased, I lost all hope.

'In the shooting club I'd sneaked into for masochistic reasons, I had a lucky break. You arrived! I identified with you as soon as I saw the sad loneliness in your face. I thanked my destiny for sending me this innocent young man whose father I'd shot. I was honoured by your interest in me, and when I heard you were also the victim of an unhappy marriage, my heart broke. But I thought I saw a light at the end of the tunnel for you. When I decided to take you under my wing my life was to recover some temporary meaning.

'On the course once, when I saw how uneasy you were, I left you alone in the room and slipped into the dressing room. It wasn't the first time I opened your locker, but rummaging in the pocket of your jacket I found a note threatening you, and I kept close to you for seventy-two hours. While you were asleep in your bed my assistant Asım and I took turns at the bend of the road opposite your main gate to keep watch from his car. I also realized that for the first time I didn't mind breaking my oath when I shot the wretched man who attacked you on the edge of the Ottoman cemetery. I think I punished the scum guilty of İz's traffic accident as you would have wished. Otherwise they would never be brought to justice.

'If you'd said, "I want them dead," your word would have been law, Arda!

'I don't know how many I've gunned down. I'm ashamed to have turned into an incorrigible killing-machine. I refuse to take refuge in a system of justice which fails to recognize its own famous sultan's tomb or the gravestones of its veteran pashas. Suicide's not an option for a fighting warrior, but you, Arda, can put an end to this misery!

'When I unlock your handcuffs and put the old Webley in your hand, you must aim for my heart. In films they count to ten but I'll wait till twenty. When I say *twenty* pull the trigger and put the gun in my right hand. For a convincing scenario there's even a suicide note in my shirt pocket. If you think firing one bullet is too much for your father's sick assassin, may I ask this favour: in one go get rid of your desire for revenge and save your own life at one and the same time?

'Otherwise, even if I regretted it later, I have a duty to perform according to the rules of my world. When you aim the Webley at my heart, I'll direct my gun at yours. If I'm alive, Arda, you can't live! I don't want to live with the fear of a future raid on my humble home. I have two dozen witnesses in hell who can swear I'm not bluffing when there's a gun in my hand. One last word: if you don't pull the trigger, someone else surely will ...'

He undid my handcuffs with an apologetic expression and put a thin beige glove on my right hand. Then he gave me the Webley, which took a single bullet. He turned on his portable radio and found a station playing mournful music. His eyes shone as his left hand took a revolver from his plastic bag. He pulled his armchair over until we were knee to knee and smiled wryly as he guided my gun-barrel to touch his heart. As his gun-barrel touched my heart my hair stood on end. Before he began to count, he said, 'If you're lucky there's one more clue. I've put my diary in your bag.'

Now numbers began to drop from his lips like prayers. When he reached 'FIVE' I started to sweat.

– SIX

(I was curious to know when I'd begin to see my whole life pass before my eyes like a film-strip.)

– SEVEN

(Might my father's ghost be watching this postmodern duel which would be ended by numbers?)

– EIGHT

(I remembered the centenary of Elias Canetti, that authentic Ottoman maker of aphorisms.)

– NI-I-NE

(Paul Cezanne declared, 'The painter must observe like a dog, with eyes fixed and forbidding.')

– TENN…

(As my fear of coming face to face with Bedirhan Cahid subsided, I stopped sweating.)

– ELEVEN

(It seemed he too was pleased with this position.)

– TWELVE

(Remembering sentences from Küçük İskender's manifesto, 'Everyone Must Have a Corpse,' I regretted that I never asked Selçuk Altun to introduce me.)

– THIRTEEN

'For the last few minutes I've been feeling uneasy that I've had to plan and carry out a crime of murder in one hour. If I'd begun to plan it long ago I would certainly have messed it up.'

– FOURTEEN

'As history is always under revision it's more difficult to look out for the ideal moment. The perfect crime is committed by chance. It's improvised.'

– FIFTEE-EN…

'A crime requires courage, strength, the right weapon and of course a live victim (if possible a human being).'

– SIXTEEN!

'It's nearly midnight and now that I'm becoming a murderer I'm happy. An indescribable joy fills my heart.'

– SEVENTEEN!

'Now I can be proud to be among people. And if I can't, even dreaming of it is a comfort.'

– EIGHTEEN!

(As Bedirhan began to frown I remembered the diary in the old plastic bag. My being was overwhelmed by the desire to possess it.)

– NINETEE-EE-N!

Suddenly I remembered my mother saying, 'You have such a silly expression on your face, Arda, that Italians in Venice and Scotsmen in London will spot a victim and ask you for directions.' I couldn't bear her coming between us, accusing me of weakness and squealing like a child. Very slowly, as though I was stroking a thoroughbred's rump, I pulled the trigger of the Webley as Cahid Hodja had ordered, and released it. As my mother's ghost evaporated I came face to face with the corpse of my father's killer. I thought I saw him laughing for the first time. I turned off his primitive radio. I thrust the old Webley into his right hand according to his instructions, and put the gun that fell from his hand into the plastic bag along with his diary. I was exhausted. For some reason I stood without moving behind the main door, the plastic bag in my hand. My mother used to say, 'Don't rush out of the shower till all the water's run off you.' (I knew I was about to be free of her ghost forever.)

Deserted Eşrefsaat was as innocent as a Fellini film-set waiting eagerly for morning. As I turned into Parlak Street I wondered if Asım would know when he returned to his master's house that he had planned this suicide.

'He's an Orphan Now' were the words written over the boot of the taxi I hailed in Şemsi Paşa Avenue. Between the two thick volumes I took gently from the plastic bag I found a goodbye note:

Dear Arda,

Well done! I hope your dreams never become nightmares because of me.

We were both the victims of marriages that began with love but ended in hatred. Because of this earth there cannot be a heaven. There is no escape from alternate states of heaven and hell, birth and death.

It was not possible to ask my nervy Gürsel Ergene Hodja to solve the problem of how to transport to heaven those who have finished their punishment in hell. I wish I could remember who told me there was a great library in purgatory for the gang of philosophers, poets and writers …

Your fellow conspirator,

B.

If Gürsel Ergene was the angry man whose photograph resembled my father, should I have been afraid because his name rhymed with Mürsel? I very much wanted to plunge into Bedirhan's diary before I went home if only the driver with the bushy moustache wouldn't turn round to look. I knew I would find İfakat in the sitting room dozing in front of a film. I entered my office and hid the diary among the rare books on Istanbul – to study closely at the first opportunity. I checked the magazine and barrel of the automatic gun and crammed it into the bottom of my briefcase, intending to get rid of it. It didn't contain a single bullet ...

CR

Having just commited the second murder in Eşrefsaat, I was shattered by news of my uncle's death. On my way to collect his body, İz spoke to me on the phone, 'I want to let you know that last night I dreamt you were attacked by a half-black, half-white man waving a scimitar and you killed him with a gun your mother handed to you at the last minute.'

Adil Kasnak came with me. Reading Bedirhan's diary, I was comforted by this massive man sitting next to me who, whenever he wasn't muttering, was snoring heavily. I didn't cry for my uncle whom I'd never seen weep even for his own mother's death. My last relative, who never thought evil of anyone in his whole life, had met his unusual death a little sooner than he expected. On the

way back to Istanbul, his co-traveller Gun told me that
he was following a snow leopard and her two cubs when
he slipped and fell into a crevasse twenty metres deep.
When they took him from the morgue I realized I hadn't
ever seen him with his eyes closed. He looked as if he was
waiting to see the end of his dream. He seemed at ease, like
a civil servant on his way home with his pay, dozing off on
a public bus. I couldn't help thinking that if grandfather
had seen the hundreds who attended his funeral, from
businessman to kebab-house owner, from tour guide to
betting-shop runner, he would most certainly have been
annoyed. For the first time in my life, I felt proud of a
family member as I held back my tears and saw humanity
grieving for Salvador Taragano, the man who had left me
almost all his wealth while he was still alive.

I knew I would get caught up in Bedirhan's diary and
finish it on the Istanbul–Katmandu–Istanbul trip. I read
all the way through this wasted life. Although a painful
inner world had been concealed under a blanket of external
dilemmas, nevertheless he had managed to enjoy travelling
to exotic climates. The possibility that his grandfather
had shot mine, Baki's dollar-oriented death trade, and the
fact that the address of a pervert who ended up as victim
instead of hunter had been given to enter a competition in
which Bedirhan used the diary of a suicidal writer looked
as meaningless as a cartoon without a caption. It was as
if the joy of finding his future Angel of Death when we
first met was concealed by his line, 'I've found A.' (I never

recalled meeting him on my visits to Dalga.) I guessed he had sold the remainder of his books at nominal prices to secondhand book dealers he didn't know.

Reading between the lines, it was clear he had consigned the wellbeing of eccentric Gürsel Ergene to me. I went to the hospital wondering if I would meet a devil in disguise, only to learn that he had committed suicide the same day as Bedirhan.

'May he rest in peace, he seems to have suffocated himself with a paper bag he made out of pages torn from his diary,' said the hard-boiled nurse. I told İz everything that happened, apart from Bedirhan's unloaded gun. When I gulped and said, 'You have listened to secrets a man would tell only to his wife, so now you must marry me,' she caressed my cheeks with both hands and said, 'Not a bad idea, Arda. I'm pregnant.'

At first I was embarrassed like a young boy whose circumcised penis is on show for the first time in a women's Turkish bath! Then I sensed the explosion of fireworks in every cell in my body cells. I embraced İz but and then made for the ridges of Çamlıca. I was thankful for the abundance of smells in the deserted streets and for the existence of an earth I had begun to sense again. Following a tumbling wind I turned into peaceful Huzur Street. I leaned back against an old weeping willow, my hands behind me, as the sound of the mosques in the background arose for the noon ezan. Very slowly I closed my eyes. I watched my life go by like a film, but from the end back to the beginning. Even when a playful thought occurred to me, I didn't open my eyes. I had to ask Selçuk Altun – I was going to give him Bedirhan's diary after censoring it – to find me a good classical guitar teacher. Cahid Hodja, may he rest in heaven, used to say, 'Your hand suits a gun, you'd make a good musician.'

I thought that only film stars shed tears with their eyes shut.